j
C.l

Lawson, John
    If pigs could fly.   Houghton
Mifflin Co., 1989.
    [136] p.

1. United States - History - War of
1812 - Fiction. I. Title.

50361288   88-35974/13.95/490

6/90

If Pigs
Could
Fly

If Pigs Could Fly

John Lawson

Houghton Mifflin Company
Boston   1989

Library of Congress Cataloging-in-Publication Data

Lawson, John (John Shults)
    If pigs could fly / John Lawson.
      p.   cm.
    Summary: Relates the adventures of Morgan James who, on his way
to find a preacher so he can marry Annabel Lee, finds himself involved
in a series of events climaxing with helping General Andrew Jackson win
an important battle against the British at New Orleans in 1815.
    ISBN 0–395–50928–9
   ✓[1. United States—History—War of 1812—Fiction. 2. Humorous stories.]
I. Title.
PZ7.L43827If   1989   88–35974
[Fic]—dc19   CIP
                AC

Printed in the United States of America

P   10 9 8 7 6 5 4 3 2 1

"It was good of you to come,
Morgan James," General Andrew Jackson
said. "We need men like you, sir."
The Battle of New Orleans
could now begin.

For
Charlotte Whalen
and for
Jack Whalen

1.

The pedlar came every Spring in his horse and wagon
to the mountains of Virginia with all sorts of things
like pots and pans and calico. There were syrups, and
balms for cow teats, and elixirs for female ailments
and for the bowels and for the back and rejuvenation,
too. And that Spring, Morgan James went with him.

He got on the high seat of the van behind the old
horse and the spring world stretched out before them
full of promise and apple blossoms.

They spent a long time at Mrs. Gwylym's. She was
a round red-cheeked lady who looked like an apple,
and what she wanted most was the bolt of red calico
she had ordered a year ago and her cough syrup. She
bought a gallon of it every year. In the beginning it
was for her children's colic and now it was for her.
And she took needles and thread and buttons, and her
husband took tobacco, but no spirits. He looked long-
ingly at the rum, but he took none.

"There will be no spirits in this house, Mr. Gwylym," said Mrs. Gwylym. And that was that.

There was a particular straw hat she wanted which Dr. Coffin — which was what the pedlar was called — didn't have because of the blockade. He was called Dr. Coffin because all his medicines had Dr. Coffin's name on them — the cough syrup, and the consumption syrup, and the colic syrup, and the female ailments syrup, and the iron syrup, and the bowel syrup. He had bottles in the back of the van where he could find almost anything for anything that ailed man-and-woman-kind and beasts, too, like foot-rot and ticks and worms and pinkeye. It was all in the back of the van and it was a wonder he could have so many different cures for so many different ailments in the back of one small van. But he did.

They took the order for the hat and for some gunpowder for Mr. Gwylym. Before they left, Mrs. Gwylym took another gallon of the syrup — in case. When they left, they left Mrs. Gwylym half draped in her new red calico, which made her look more like an apple than ever. She was sipping her cough syrup and Mr. Gwylym was kicking the dust.

There was a place along the road where there was a good spring and they stopped there because Dr. Coffin had to make up more of his famous syrup. They made a fire and they took the big copper pot and they put water in it and cherries and slips of sassafras (for congestion) and laurel leaves (for headaches) and wild red rhubarb stalks and a honeycomb and blackstrap molasses (so some of the bottles could be labeled Spring Tonic) and lots of sugar. Morgan James stirred it with a locust stick. And they boiled it, and boiled it, and boiled it until the bark came off the stick and the wood became white. Then they strained it through the burlap bag the cherries had been in until the burlap rotted and then they stirred it some more.

"Now, boy," said Dr. Coffin, "let's see how good you are at arith-metics. We have about three gallons of essence there and we want that to be one-tenth of the total mixture. So how much rum do we add?"

"Alcohol? You going to put alcohol in it?"

"I am going to put alcohol in it, boy. Do you think any lady would pay good money for this goo as it is? Do you think so? If you believe that, boy, you'll believe that pigs can fly."

"But alcohol! What would Mrs. Gwylym say! She doesn't approve of spirits." Morgan James was really really shocked.

Dr. Coffin was busy measuring out the alcohol. "Fifteen . . . sixteen . . . seventeen . . . eighteen — quiet, I'm counting. There — twenty-seven gallons of alcohol. That does it."

"But," said Morgan James, "suppose Mrs. Gwylym knew, suppose she knew she was drinking all these spirits?"

"Maybe she does know and maybe she doesn't want to know and maybe she knows but doesn't want to tell herself and maybe she doesn't believe it could be spirits because she knows how she feels about spirits and that's pretty positive — I mean to say negative. There are possibilities, boy, beyond conjuring up. And now we have to get this stuff into bottles fast before it evaporates like a late frost."

They poured it into dark brown bottles and corked them. "Don't spill it," Dr. Coffin warned. "It will take the skin off." They labeled the bottles with DR. COFFIN labels — Cough Syrup, Spring Tonic, Female Elixir, Rejuvenol, and Bowel Bomb, and Liver Extract. Then they put some in some very, very small black bottles with a label that just said Excelsior and had cherubs chasing each other.

"What's this for?" said Morgan James. "They're so small."

"It's for whatever you think might ail you. Or it ails you and you don't know what it is. And that's why it comes in such small precious bottles. They sell for three dollars. And the big ones sell for fifty cents."

"But it's the same thing," said Morgan James. "The same darned thing."

"The big ones aren't called Excelsior, are they?"

They spent the night under a kind of awning that came out from the end of the van and it was very nice. It was cool but they could hear the foxes barking and some lambs crying way off. It was perfect. And Morgan James swore to himself that he would stay

4

with Dr. Coffin awhile and learn peddling. He told him that the next morning. He could tell that it pleased Dr. Coffin, because Dr. Coffin hardly said anything except, "You're welcome. You're a good sort even if you are an innocent. And if you don't die of misadventure before your time perhaps you'll be all right."

"I'm not planning on that anyway," said Morgan James as he turned over some of Mrs. Gwylym's eggs in the frying pan. "If I'm going to stay with you I should know what your real name is."

"Why do you say that? It says it on the bottle, don't it?"

"That's what I mean." Morgan James had been stung by that remark about his innocence. He put the fried eggs inside one of Mrs. Gwylym's biscuits.

"Well, it happens you're right. I did it for business reasons."

"But if I were going to do that — change my name from Morgan James, which I am attached to — if I was about to do that for business reasons and if I was in your business, I would take a name like Dr. Good-feel or Dr. Feelgood — something like that. Dr. Coffin is spooky-sounding."

Then Morgan James went back to his biscuit, which had started to come apart during his long speech.

Dr. Coffin sipped some of his liver tonic. His liver usually bothered him in the morning from sleeping on the ground. "It's a good idea," said Dr. Coffin.

"I knew I could be helpful," said Morgan James.

"Which do you like best — Dr. Goodfeel or Dr. Feel-good?"

"Except it won't work."

"What won't work?" The sun was well up now and especially on Morgan James right where the eggs and biscuits fitted in. He was really sleepy and wasn't thinking very fast. "What won't work?"

"Your idea. Tried it years ago. Called myself Dr. Smilenow. And was happy. And smiled all the time. And the customers were happy. My Lord, they were happy and healthy with not one ailment per thousand. Did they buy extracts or balms or elixirs? They never bought nothing. So I gave it up. And took up Dr. Coffin. And started talking low and mournful. You know how I talk. And it comes across like 'We're all in this together, boys. We're headed for the grave.' That did it. Put fear in their hearts, Morgan James, shook 'em to their foundations. And I had to fight 'em off. The elixirs moved like sparks out of a pine knot. Folks were ailing. They were sick all right."

"That's amazing," said Morgan James and got up to see if he could shift Mrs. Gwylym's biscuits around to where they would be more comfortable.

"That's my only reservation about your coming with me," said Dr. Coffin as he rolled up the awning. "You're too healthy. Your appetite's too good. Now if you could get consumption we could make a fortune."

"I could try," said Morgan James and pulled in his

pink cheeks, but he didn't really look sick, even though Mrs. Gwylym's biscuits were helping.

The night mist was still rising from the valley as they took to the road that morning. The trees half leaved were still threatening, spooky shapes and not yet trees and limbs. And as if reminded, Dr. Coffin said that they were coming to Indian country soon. Morgan James pulled his rifle closer to him.

"There will be no shooting, Morgan James. It aggravates them. And besides you might hit one. And that would fire them up."

"But what do we do if they come?" said Morgan James without letting go of his rifle.

"We out-strategize them."

"Look, there's a house over there. Way over there," said Morgan James, nodding to where you could just see a house and a roll of white-gray smoke rising. "Aren't we going to stop there?"

"We don't stop there," said Dr. Coffin without even looking over.

"Why's that?"

"Used to stop there. There was a girl there then. But she's probably not still a girl, because she was even beginning to bud then. No, she's not the most miserable girl in the world anymore I ever knew. She's probably the most miserable woman in the world I ever didn't know, and I'm going to leave it that way."

"Even if she's awful, she could still make good biscuits. That smoke coming up that chimney could be coming from the biscuits she's making right now."

"A buzzard would die if it ate a biscuit made by Annabel Lee. We're not stopping," said the Doctor.

"You must know her pretty well, then," said Morgan James.

"She's redheaded, for one thing," said Dr. Coffin, "and I don't know why, but it's a never-failing sign — the redheaded female at all costs is to be avoided. Remember that, Morgan James, avoid the redheaded female at all costs. And now that she's a full-budded woman the thought of a confrontation makes my blood run cold."

Morgan James looked over to the house where the smoke was rolling up out of the chimney. "She must be making biscuits for the whole week."

"Her ambition knows no bounds," said Dr. Coffin. "She must have it in mind to poison the whole country this time."

"What I want to know is what she did to you."

"She almost burnt me alive is what she did to me. Burnt the house down around me, or at least one end of the house. I used to go there, as I said, and I was having a night-over, sleeping by the fire in the kitchen. Like I said, I was sleeping, and she came down the stairs on tiptoe in her short white shift with her red pigtails and her brown legs like a fawn's. They're probably like fence posts now. But they were pretty

8

then. Anyway, she went on tiptoe into my saddlebag and took out an Excelsior bottle. I should of stopped her then and there but I wanted to see what she was a-going to do. God help me, I should of known it was going to be something horrendous. But I had no idea how horrendous. She slipped up to the fire on those brown deer legs and — and she threw the Excelsior bottle in the fire. In the fire, mind you. And then she was gone and just as well, because if the explosion hadn't gotten her I would have. It steamed and hissed and sizzled, and before I could collect myself it exploded. And Vesuvius was nothing to it. There was no smoke. There was just fire. And then the chimney caught. Have you ever seen a chimney fire? I mean a real chimney fire where it rumbles and roars and gulps air like a congestive whale. The whole house shook. And she comes down the stairs with her mother. 'I told you it was spirits,' she said. 'Spirits. Pure spirits.' She had been saying all day that I put spirits in my pharmaceuticals — which she had no right to say. To prove her wrong I had poured a very special — you understand — bottle on the fire to show her wrong, which it did, and I guess it mightily aggravated her so she had done this for revenge. Mean, spiteful, hateful, miserable revenge, Morgan James. Don't ever become poisoned by revenge, Morgan James."

"I wouldn't touch one of her biscuits," said Morgan James. "Probably like rocks."

"Nothing we could do but let the fire burn itself

out, and all she did was dance around in that short white shift on those brown deer legs shouting 'Spirits! Spirits! I told you it was spirits!' — like a banshee with red pigtails, if you can imagine that."

"It's lucky it wasn't one of those big fifty-cent bottles," said Morgan James.

"We'd have been gone — all of us would have been gone," said Dr. Coffin, "and that's why we're not stopping."

"It's reason enough," said Morgan James, and looked no more at the house where the smoke was puffing low in a gray and white spiral.

They were coming now to a dark pine forest where the sun only dappled through, and it was still and silent where they were but the wind was above in the trees and sounded like the sea. "It's Indian country if I ever saw one," said Dr. Coffin, pulling his hat tight.

"It's such Indian country that I just saw one — over there," said Morgan James.

"And there's twenty more for every one you see."

"I can hear them," said Morgan James, as calm as could be.

"They're multiplying fast," said Dr. Coffin. "Count again."

"Twenty-one," said Morgan James, looking around.

"You counted too fast. Count slowly this time," said Dr. Coffin.

"I don't have to. I saw one and then I added in the

twenty I couldn't see like you said and that makes twenty-one."

"We're coming to a nice straight stretch of road where we're going to strategize them."

The Indians were beginning to whoop now. "*Whoop! Whoop!*" There were so many that Morgan James could not keep adding twenty on every time he saw one as they flitted through the trees whooping — "*Whoop! Whoop!*"

"Here's how," said the doctor. "Up there by that big rock I'm going to stop and you're going to take a half jug — half, mind you — of rum and walk back with it down the road very slowly and then you're going to put it down in the middle of the road and then you're going to walk back here slowly — and then we're going to skedaddle."

"I'm going to do that?" said Morgan James.

"Slowly. The trick is the slowly."

"I think you could do it better than I could," said Morgan James.

"I'd get nervous and couldn't go as slow as you."

"And you'll wait? You won't skedaddle afore time?"

"And leave you at the mercy of those whooping savages, Morgan James!" He put his hand like a father on Morgan James' shoulder.

"I'll do it," said Morgan James.

"There's a half jug in the corner, and there's the big rock where I'm going to stop. Now remember: slowly, don't look back, about a hundred yards and then back to me — and we'll be off slick as a whistle."

"I'll do it," said Morgan James.

It went fine — at first. He took the jug and started back down the road. That one Indian walked through the pines along with him. And the twenty shadows came along too, flitting from tree to tree. Morgan James wanted very much to whistle to show them what he thought of them but no whistle came. He had almost gone what must have been the one hundred yards when he heard a *"Har! Har! Haree!"* and it was Dr. Coffin standing in the seat of the wagon flailing at the old horse, who was going into his first gallop in years, with pots and pans rattling.

"Dr. Coffin! Dr. Coffin!" shouted Morgan James. "You forgot me! You forgot me!

"It must have been that Dr. Coffin couldn't hear above the pots and pans," said Morgan James to himself. "That must be why he didn't stop."

Morgan James ran after him as fast as he could. And then he dropped the jug and the rum went all over the road. Then the whooping started again — *"Whoop! Whoop!"* — and then they were after him. All of them. Lots of them. And there were more than twenty-one.

Morgan James took off through the woods on the side of the road where he hoped there weren't any Indians. But the ones on the other side of the road came after him whooping dreadfully and it sounded as if they were saying "He broke it! He broke it!" —

but that couldn't be because Morgan James couldn't understand Indian and the Indians couldn't talk English. And they were gaining on him because they were going faster because they had all this practice chasing white men and a white man never really got practiced trying to outrun a red Indian. Morgan James knew this. It was not something he had heard, because there wasn't anyone to tell it, but he had seen some white men who had not outrun the Indians and he didn't want to be on that list. So he ran and dodged and ran and dodged until he didn't know where he was but it was not promising with those savages running and dodging behind him and whooping. And then he saw a pond the beavers had dammed. And that had promise. He had heard oncet about a man hiding from the Indians in a beaver house. It became a real possibility in his circumstances that he decided to explore. And without more thought than that, he did. He dived into the cold cold water and swam underwater toward the beaver house. There was an entrance. In it he went and squeezed inside. It was dark. It was absolutely completely dark. There was a bank, like. He crawled up out of the water. He was afraid to reach out too far for fear of the beavers. He thought he could hear them sort of breathing heavy and scratching. He didn't know who else could be in a beaver house. And it smelt like beavers, years and years of beavers in there. He crawled up farther to where there was a second story. It was drier here and now he could hear the Indians rustling around, grunting to each other. They weren't whooping at all. He had always suspected that that whooping was just for showoff and that they didn't do it amongst themselves.

It seemed they had gone away, because the grunting stopped. There was only the sound of the heavy breathing and the scratching of the beavers on the floor below him. Every once in a while one would slap his tail the way they do. Then Morgan James found out why they breathed so heavily and scratched and slapped their tails, because what was biting them was biting him. Small sharp bites, except it went on burning where these things, whatever they were, bit oncet and then moved on to fresher territory until it seemed like he must be on fire. He couldn't stand up but he could kneel, peeling off his clothes so the varmints wouldn't have a place to put their feet and get their teeth in so well. It did not work. It just exposed new fresh possibilities for them. He was sure that they were leaving the beavers downstairs to come up to him since he was a novelty.

He thought he heard a beaver slip into the water below him and he longed to get into the water himself. It was certainly something that had growing appeal. Even the Indians couldn't be as bad as these things eating him alive, which he wouldn't be very long at the rate it was going.

Then he heard this voice, the most sweet wondrous

voice in this world — or maybe these things had bit him into the next. Anyway, it was a sweet voice telling a story which must have had a beginning which Morgan James had not heard because the teller was already in the middle of the tale. "There I was, Bess, at the top of the stairs. This long long curving stair with the music playing. And I came down. The stairs were so long that when I was at the bottom of the stairs the hem of my skirt was still upstairs. Can you imagine, Bess? Can you imagine that?" Bess didn't say anything. This girl, whoever she was who was talking, wouldn't be dressed like that if she were on the same story where Morgan James was, he thought. "Then, Bess, listen to this. A dragoon comes to the foot of the stairs where I'm standing, twirling the biggest moustache you have ever seen and I felt like he was twirling my heart — 'Annabel Lee, I presume!' "

Morgan James would have liked to hear how it came out in the end, but it was more than time to leave forthwith. If this girl in the long gown was there and Bess was there, then it followed pretty clearly that there weren't any Indians there. As he slipped into the water he heard her say, "Now stop it, Bess, or you'll go right home. Stop it this minute."

The water was still cold and he got out of it as fast as he could. There was a girl there — a woman really — and a cow. And she, the woman, had red hair. Morgan James knew it was not his day. First the

Indians. Then the bugs in the beaver house. Then falling naked into the hands of a red-haired woman after all that Dr. Coffin had warned him.

"Are you an Anabaptist?" she said.

"I am not an Anabaptist," said Morgan James.

"I thought you might be. There are some over the mountain and they say they go around like you."

"I have escaped from the Indians," said Morgan James very firmly.

"Pooh," she said. "The Indians around here wouldn't hurt a fly."

"They gave a pretty good imitation."

"Why do you keep scratching?"

"It was the bugs in the beaver house."

"That's what you get for going in there. And I suppose you left your clothes in there."

"It was the bugs," said Morgan James.

"First it's the Indians and then it's the bugs. Are you sure you're not an Anabaptist?"

"I don't even know what an Anabaptist is."

"It's a sect — S-E-C-T — that lives over the mountain and they don't wear clothes and I can't take you home if you are one because my mother does not approve of them one whit."

"Your mother is right," said Morgan James. "No one more approves of clothes than I do."

Annabel Lee — because it must have been she — turned Bess around from the beaver pond and they started home. Bess went first. Then Morgan James.

Then the red-haired girl called Annabel Lee.

"They bit you on the back side, too," she said, as if she approved of the thoroughness.

"They're not choosy." He wished he could see her on the stairs someday in that long gown with bugs inside.

"Dr. Coffin's liniment will fix you up."

"Not on me," said Morgan James. "It takes the skin off."

"He tried to burn our house down, you know. Don't stop, Bess, keep going!" Bess kept going, not fast, but going. They did not usually go home quite this early but she did keep going.

Annabel Lee stopped. "And how long were you in that beaver house?"

"Hours and hours. Maybe days and days." It was her sympathy he wanted more than anything in the world.

"Now turn around. Look at me. I want to know what you heard me say to Bess. Sometimes I talk to Bess when I walk her and I want to know what you heard. Put your hand on your heart! You know I can see it. There will be no flubbery about where your heart is. So what did you hear?"

Morgan James thought fast, maybe faster than he had ever thought. " 'Stop it Bess,' you said, 'or I'll take you home.' "

"That's all you heard? Now cross your big toe and say, 'I swear that's all.' "

"I swear that's all," said Morgan James, feeling the

17

fool but knowing it was the right thing to do.

Bess walked slowly without even looking for a path that would be better for Morgan James' bare feet. He wondered how long this day could be.

"And if you don't stop scratching you won't have any skin left where I'm looking, Dr. Coffin's liniment or not."

"Then stop looking," said Morgan James. He almost added "Annabel Lee" but he caught himself before he gave the game away.

The cabin was a nice trim one and it looked as warm and inviting to Morgan James as any cabin he had ever seen. There was no doubt that it was the cabin he had seen from the road where Dr. Coffin had said that red-headed girl lived who was now behind him. She was no girl anymore and her legs were not like fence posts either.

A firm no-nonsense lady came out on the steps — and looked first at Bess, then at Morgan James, and then at Annabel Lee. "And what have you got there, Annie?"

"Annabel Lee, if you please, Momma. And he's no Anabaptist!"

The mother came and looked Morgan James over closely as if deciding whether to send him back whence he came. "Anabaptist or not, he's been bit till he looks like a raspberry."

"He was in a beaver house, Momma."

"He's a man grown and he's no business in a beaver

house at his age. And beavers don't bite like that. If pigs could fly!"

"Of course not," said Morgan James. He was getting cold from the evening air coming down the mountain and he was hot and shivery from the bites. "It was the bugs that were on the beavers, ma'am."

"Then you have done the beavers a great favor, because by the looks of you there are no more bugs on the beavers. Do you have a name?"

"Morgan James, ma'am."

"Then sit down on the steps, Morgan James, and Annie will get some hot vinegar water and we'll put you in a tub and soak you till you're wrinkled like a pickle."

"Out here? I want to come in. I'm cold."

"Out here. I don't pretend to understand your fervor for beaver houses and it's not here nor there, but this is no beaver house, Morgan James, no matter how it may look to your inflamed mind."

Morgan James sat and shivered until his heels were making drumbeats on the step. Nor did he want to be wrinkled like a pickle. The wrinkling might just be permanent and his fair white skin which he was very attached to might never smooth out and he would be old before his time. It was not promising. She might know a lot about pickles but he didn't know how much she knew about his fair white skin. He would have left. He would have taken off then and there except they came out with the tub. Annabel Lee poured in the hot water. Her mother poured in the vinegar as though it was water.

"Get in," she said and went back inside for more vinegar.

"I'm not getting in," said Morgan James, almost overwhelmed by the steaming vinegar. "I'm leaving. I am going to flee."

"He won't go in the tub, Momma!" Annabel screamed. "He says he is going to flee!"

"He'll go in!" said her mother, coming out. She took him by the hair and led him to the tub.

"You are pulling out my locks, ma'am. They will never grow back!" Now he was going to be bald as well as wrinkled. But he stepped in and sat down with his knees under his chin. He would save them at least.

"Pour this pot over him, Annie, so we get his head done too."

Annabel Lee did it with an enthusiasm that was uncalled for. When the water got cool she poured on more hot water. When the vinegar lost its vigor she poured in more vinegar. If the bugs felt the way he did they were dead or expiring.

He was weak. He was steamed. He was wrinkled, but he was not going to die in that tub. He was going to die on dry land.

But Annabel Lee pushed him back in. "You can't get out like that. You're naked."

"I got in naked and I'm going to get out naked."

"He's getting out, Momma! And he's naked!" she screamed.

Her mother came out with fresh clothes. "Don't you dare get out of that tub naked in front of Annabel Lee. My daughter is an upstanding modest maid."

"See," said Annabel Lee and stuck out her tongue at him.

But it was too late. It had taken Morgan James' last strength to make that first move. He was too weak now. He began to sink. The mother sent Annabel Lee inside and pulled Morgan James out by his remaining hair and let him sink in a soggy wrinkled lump on the floor. "When you're proper you can come in," and she went in.

Morgan James never knew how he was able to put on his new deerskin pants and deerskin jacket with deerskin tassels, but he did.

"I've never seen you with clothes on," said Annabel Lee. "Even if you smell like a pickle you're not scratching anymore."

"I'm too weak to scratch," whispered Morgan James. But it was true. He wasn't itching anymore. He looked at his hands. His fair white skin was whiter than ever and was smoothing out. He couldn't even smell the vinegar.

Annabel Lee put him in the rocker by the fire. Her mother brought hot potato soup and salted deer steak and biscuits with rhubarb preserves. It had been a good day. It had been one of Morgan James' best days. Red hair or not, he was going to stay here. He was never going to leave, to leave, to . . .

He fell asleep right there in the rocker. They put him down in front of the fire when they went to bed. He never woke or stirred.

"Beaver house indeed," said Annabel Lee's mother. "If pigs could fly!"

2.

Breakfast was too much, even by Morgan James' standards. There was oatmeal, bacon and eggs, buckwheat cakes and sausage and maple syrup and biscuits. Annabel Lee cooked them all and brought them to him steaming.

When he was finished and about to burst he noticed how pretty she looked with her hair all combed and a white frilly blouse. "You must be going someplace," he said.

"I am not going, as you say, Morgan James, anyplace."

Morgan James would have liked to put on the boots Annabel Lee's mother had found for him, but he could not bend over. He was too full. He decided to change the subject to one which would be universally acceptable. "I suppose you got dressed up because you saw how handsome I am in my deerskin jacket and deer-skin pants all with deerskin tassels. Why do you look like that? Don't I look right? Have you got a mirror? I want to see myself."

Annabel Lee slammed down the dish she was carry-ing and ran out of the room. "What's wrong with her?" Morgan James said to Annabel Lee's mother.

"I have no idea if you don't."

"She was eating awful fast," said Morgan James. He was looking forward to a day when nothing would happen — not good or bad, not fortunate or horren-dous, just a quiet day when the sun went down at its appointed hour and the moon came up punctually without complications. One of those days.

"I suppose you like the way I look now." It was Annabel Lee at the top of the stairs. She apparently had a fondness for the tops of stairs. She had on a long black shawl with gloves to the elbow and a long skirt and long pants underneath and netting over head and face — all kind of tied together with rope.

"If you are trying to fright me, you have," said Morgan James.

"Why don't you ask me if I am going someplace?"

"Wherever that place might be they wouldn't let you in."

"That's Annie's bee-hunting outfit," said her mother proudly. "She made it herself."

"You don't hunt bees, they hunt you," he said.

Annabel Lee handed Morgan James an ax.

24

"You want me to cut you out of that outfit already?"

"The ax is to cut down the limb."

Morgan James was beginning to have that sinking feeling that it was not going to be one of those days when the sun and the moon and all living creatures were behaved. "What limb?"

Annabel Lee shook her head in exasperation. "The limb that the beehive is on, of course."

"You mean I am going to cut down a limb with a beehive on it?"

"Now you understand."

"I won't do it. I am going to stay here. I have things to do. I have to watch the sun go down and I have to watch the moon go up."

Annabel Lee took off her bee bonnet and came very close to Morgan James. She took one of the deerskin tassels in her hand. "For me," she said.

"I'll do it," said Morgan James.

"I'll need my sugar water, Momma," said Annabel Lee, "and I'll take this saucer."

"You cannot take that one, Annie, it matches the one you lost last time. Take this one."

"It's cracked."

"I don't think the bees will notice. And don't forget your burlap bag and remember to keep that netting tight over your head."

"I don't have any netting to keep tight over my head," said Morgan James.

"Annie is wonderful with the bees," said Annabel

Lee's mother, putting a cork in the sugar-water jug.

"It's because I am such a simple pure soul that they trust me. I talk to them in nature's own sweet tongue," said Annabel Lee.

There was nothing to be said after that. They gathered their things — the ax, the burlap bag, the twine for the burlap bag, the sugar water, the cracked saucer, and copper teakettles with coals — and set off toward the woods.

"This is a good place," said Annabel Lee when they reached the middle of the meadow where the red clover was the heaviest in bloom. She put the saucer down and poured sugar water in it. "I would have liked the other saucer. It had flowers on it. I know the bees would have liked it better."

"Are we just going to sit here?" said Morgan James.

"I have noticed you have no patience," said Annabel Lee.

"I don't see anything happening. I don't even know what to look for that's going to happen."

"It's happening now," said Annabel Lee. "I can feel it. You are saying to yourself that you are now alone on this morning in this meadow with Annabel Lee, and all the things that you have wanted to say to her are boiling up inside of you ready to pour out. Talk!" She took off her bee bonnet and the netting and lay back on the grass with her red hair about her shoulders and her eyes closed. "Talk!" she said.

"I just saw a bee go in the saucer," said Morgan

James. Annabel Lee did not answer. She had the bee bonnet and netting on again and was sitting up.

"Are you all right?" said Morgan James. "You're making strange sounds."

"I am grinding my teeth. Do you mind?"

"I just saw another one," said Morgan James. He knew she was angry because he was spotting the bees ahead of her.

"Well, watch where they go!"

"What do you mean — watch where they go?"

"We're not out here to soak in the beauty of the morning, Morgan James. I knew I should have left you in the beaver house," said Annabel Lee, smoothing wrinkles that Morgan James couldn't see out of her skirt.

There was no call for her to be that angry on a morning like this, thought Morgan James. So he just watched the bees. They perched on the side of the sugar-water saucer and drank like horses, then heavy-loaded struggled into the air and toward the woods. But he wasn't going to tell her.

"I see now," said Annabel Lee. "Let's go."

"And where's that?" said Morgan James, getting the ax and the burlap bag with the twine.

"We follow them as far as we can see, and then we put the saucer down again, and then we find the hive."

"The hive may be in Massachusetts, and we'd have to go across Virginia, Maryland, New York, and Connecticut," said Morgan James.

"You forgot New Jersey and Rhode Island and besides the hive won't be that far away."

Four more times they put the saucer down and four more times they moved northerly until they came to the hive. It was as advertised — on the end of a limb too high to reach.

Annabel Lee was all business now. She surveyed the hive. She poured the still-red coals on the ground underneath the hive. Then she put wet leaves on them. The smoke began to roll up. She put on more wet leaves.

Morgan James still wasn't talking to her. He doubted if he would again.

"We're smoking them, you see," she said very patiently. "Then they get frightened and all go in the hive. That's when you go up the tree and chop down the limb."

It was as good a way to go as any, Morgan James thought. Maybe his being killed or certainly seriously injured would bring out whatever quality of mercy Annabel Lee had in her. Morgan James stood way to the side. The bees buzzed angrily around Annabel Lee in her bee outfit but she paid no attention and went on gathering wet leaves. The smoke poured up. Finally the bees went up in the hive.

"They want to protect the queen bee," said Annabel Lee. "That's all the males have to do. Just to lay down their lives for the queen bee."

Finally there were no bees around. They had all

gone up to the hive to lay down their lives. "Now you can go up," said Annabel Lee, "and don't just chop it down so it falls with a crash, because I have to put the burlap bag over the hive." Morgan James shinnied up the tree trunk. The smoke was almost suffocating. His eyes watered so he could hardly see. Every time he whomped the branch the hive buzzed angrily. He could only hope that those males in there were very loyal and protective. Even a couple that didn't really care that much could be very troublesome to him in his situation, hanging on the tree and not being able to see. But he did it. He chopped it down and gently lowered it to the ground so that Annabel Lee could put the burlap bag over the hive.

"Now that wasn't hard, was it?" said Annabel Lee. She gathered all the equipment. Morgan James carried the branch over his shoulder with the bees on the end of it buzzing angrily. Annabel Lee led the way, telling him to be careful here or there as the case might be.

It hurt him to know she didn't care about him but only about her bees.

Suddenly she shrieked and ran back toward him and threw her arms about him and he found himself suffocating in her red hair.

"A snake! They scare me to death!" She tried to get her feet off the ground.

Morgan James was scared to death. He dropped the limb. The bag burst. The hive burst. The bees were out. And probably the queen bee, too, because they were all after Morgan James, who did not have a bee bonnet or netting or long gloves. There was nothing for it but to flee, which Morgan James did — not forgetting Annabel Lee and the snake but feeling that they were not the first priority. He ran and the bees flew, down the hill, through another wood, and there at the bottom — how wonderful, how sweet — was the beaver pond. Morgan James was in just ahead of them. But every time he came up for air they attacked him.

Finally they left. That was when Annabel Lee came. "You can come out now," she said. "They've gone back to protect the queen bee. At least *they* care!"

It was a sad walk back to the house. Morgan James' head felt like a pincushion. He was wet. Annabel Lee had lost her hive and most of all her faith in Morgan James.

"And what has he done this time?" said Annabel Lee's mother when she saw him.

"He tried to go back in the beaver house, Momma."

"Well, at least this time it looks like he only got his head in," she said.

The days went by, promising with breakfast and then downhill. Morgan James fell off a roof putting on shingles. He went into quicksand digging a well. He fell off a cliff getting a wild flower for Annabel Lee. He was chased by a bull when he was fence-building.

30

He was chased by a bear when he was berrying. He saved Annabel Lee from two snakes. He never saw them, but they must have been very big and dangerous judging from how much protection she needed.

Sometimes Morgan James thought that Annabel Lee's breakfasts were not just for the stomach but for the soul. They nurtured his soul. Of course, he never told her that. She might turn it around and neglect the stomach, which had its place too.

It was after one of these real soul-satisfying breakfasts one morning that he told her that he thought they should probably get married.

"You do?" said Annabel Lee.

"Anybody who likes to cook as much as you do should have somebody near who likes to eat as much as I do," said Morgan James.

"You're not bunking together in this house without a preacher," said Annabel Lee's mother. "You must think you're back with the beavers!"

"I'm not talking about that," said Morgan James.

"I am," said Annabel Lee.

"There are no preachers around," said Morgan James. He had never mentioned any need for preachers. All he had said was that they should probably get married. He probably should have said "possibly." It was an idea that he had thrown out to see how it would be received. He hadn't even said yet that if someone else had thrown out the idea he would receive it well.

"Then you'll have to go get one," said Annabel Lee, taking away the last biscuit, which Morgan James had saved purposely till the end to soak in its final full measure of melted butter. At the beginning of breakfast he ate them too fast before the butter melted. He liked to save this one until it was fully matured.

"You can't do that," said Morgan James.

"No preacher, no biscuit," said Annabel Lee.

"He has to learn," said Annabel Lee's mother.

"Preachers come," he said. "They come down the road looking for business. You don't go get them. You don't go out on the road and shout 'Preacher! Preacher!' " Morgan James laughed at the absurdity he had conjured up. There was silence. He could hear the silence. He could feel it.

"No preacher. No biscuit," said Annabel Lee.

"All right, I will," said Morgan James. "Some rainy day when we have nothing important to do I'll go out and take a look around for a preacher. There are probably some along the river."

"Today," said Annabel Lee, hanging up her apron. She hung it up like she was doing it forever. She never hung up her apron in the early morning.

"You said it was of first importance to begin the pig house. You said the little pigs would die, the little tiny tiny pigs would die and you would die," said Morgan James, "if I didn't begin the pig house today."

"Let them die," said Annabel Lee.

*

From there it was a blur in which Morgan James played almost no part. A knapsack with a few clothes, a few biscuits, the Dr. Coffin's liniment which Annabel Lee's mother wanted to get out of the house. There was a map of Rhode Island which hardly seemed necessary since they were in Tennessee, but it was the only map in the house and it had always been said that Rhode Island was a very religious state.

And that was it. They walked him to the road and sent him south toward the river. He shook hands with Annabel Lee and her mother.

"He's probably going back to the beaver house and sulk," said Annabel Lee's mother.

Annabel Lee came up close to Morgan James — threw her arms around him and kissed him and then dropped him like a hot potato. It was the first time that she had ever kissed him when there were no snakes around and Morgan James knew it was a good indication of her feelings. "No, Momma, he's going to find a preacher."

"I'll do it," said Morgan James.

It was one of those drizzly mornings with the skies low down the mountains. He looked back. They were already out of sight. He felt like one of those tiny tiny pigs that didn't have a roof over their heads. And he was lonely. He knew that it had something to do with Annabel Lee not being there. There were some times he felt alone with Annabel Lee when she was off wherever she went in her dreamland, but he was never lonely when she was near. He was never cold. And now he was lonely, hungry, and cold. He could see how important this preacher had become for him.

He began to walk faster, not to get anywheres in particular, but at least somewheres. He had been walking up a mountain for a long time, so long that he had walked up into the clouds, which made him even more surprised to find a buggy at the top of the mountain. There was nobody in it. Just the horse and buggy. Then he heard a voice in the woods. He knew, without knowing how he knew, that this voice was really talking to the mountain. It was a powerful male voice — like a preacher's — and yet there was something yearning in it, crying in need of understanding which only the mountain and the fog could help.

"I come before you," the voice boomed. "No, no, that's not it. I stand here before you, a mother's child, as I know many of you are and will understand."

Morgan James went closer. There was this large elegant man in long topcoat and tall hat, standing majestically on a stump in a small clearing. There was no doubt he was a preacher if Morgan James had ever seen one. He knew he was just what Annabel Lee wanted, and to think he had found him so fast.

"You all know as well as I do why I am here today, why you are here today, why we are here together today. It is loneliness. How lonely have we all been when the apron strings are cut and we are cast from the nest to flutter alone in a world of cats and predators. I can

34

see some of you reaching to your eyes." He himself took out a big colored handkerchief and dabbed his own eyes.

Morgan James was so carried away that he had to say "Amen."

The speaker looked at him, but never broke his stride. "Hold your applause, please, until the end. We are fluttering fledglings in a world of vipers. I need you. I need your vote — and you need me, J. Clyde Bagful, to be your Senator again. It was five years ago that the citizens of Studgeville sent me to Washington to be your Senator, a poor country lad with only the clothes on his back. Look at me now. I come before you in silks and gabardine because — let me tell you — because I have been wallowing in the public trough, and if you send me back to Washington we will wallow together." He looked at Morgan James. "You may cheer now wildly," he said.

"Are you really a preacher?" said Morgan James.

"I regret that I am not. I am a U.S. Senator from the great state of Tennessee. I have not been called to be a man of the cloth although many have urged me to do so."

"You can preach all right," said Morgan James.

"I thank you, sir," said the Senator. "And what is your name, sir?"

"Morgan James."

"A fine name. A very fine name. Can I presume that a man of your judgment will give me your vote?"

"All I have," said Morgan James.

The Senator pulled out the biggest gold watch from his vest that Morgan James had ever seen. "I like your spirit, sir." He looked at Morgan James closely. "Are you presently occupied?"

"I am looking for a preacher."

"You are, are you? You're not in trouble?"

"I will be if I don't find one."

"We'll find you a preacher, but more importantly I'm looking for a front man right now," said the Senator.

"In front of what?" said Morgan James. As he had gotten older he had learned it was better not to be in the front of anything. It was always best to be back in the pack.

"I am beginning my campaign for re-election, and I need a man, a good man to go in ahead of me and prepare the populace for my entrance. Do you think you could handle it?"

"I think I'd better stick to finding a preacher," said Morgan James.

"Suppose I guarantee to find you a preacher?" said the Senator, getting back on the stump. "It's a nice stump, isn't it? Some of my best speeches have come when I was standing on this very stump. But what experience do you have for front man?"

"Well," said Morgan James, "I've built fence. I've chased Indians. I've cut down beehives. I've studied beaver houses."

"No. I mean commercial business. What have you

done in the world of commerce, Morgan James?"

"I've helped Dr. Coffin mix up his famous elixirs and syrups and liniments and salves and ointments. I've done that."

"And foisted them on the poor unsuspecting public?"

"They drank 'em up and rubbed themselves with it like wallowing pigs," said Morgan James.

"You're hired!" said the Senator, jumping down from the stump.

"What about the preacher?"

"I'll find you a preacher. Didn't I say I would?"

"No preacher, no front man," said Morgan James.

"You drive a hard bargain, Morgan James. You'll do fine," said the Senator. "We'll find a preacher."

Back at the buggy the Senator sorted out some posters for Morgan James. "Now these you have to put up all over town." They were posters announcing the arrival of Senator J. Clyde Bagful and his speaking in the market place at eight o'clock that night. And then there were prints — pictures — that he wanted about town.

"It looks like a Temple," said Morgan James.

"It is," said the Senator. "It is the Temple of Minerva. It is also the model for the United States Post Office which I am going to deliver lock, stock, and barrel to the people of Studgeville if they return me to the great Senate of the United States."

"I like it," said Morgan James. "Temples go a long ways."

"You don't have to tell them it's the Temple of Minerva. It's just that a Post Office should look like a Temple."

"And vice versa," said Morgan James.

The Senator looked at his watch again. "Now I have to make a detour on a mission of mercy to the house of a dear widow friend, but I will meet you at seven in the town square." He counted out a roll of bills for Morgan James. "It would be nice if there was a small cheering crowd as I come into town. Boys are very good at this. You might teach them to chant — they like that — 'Bagful! Bagful! Bagful!' Do you think you can handle that?"

"Bagful! Bagful! Bagful!" shouted Morgan James.

"You have it," said the Senator. "And one more thing. Tear down any posters you see with Scroggins' name on it. Would you vote for a man with the name of Scroggins?"

"I would not," said Morgan James, rolling up the posters under his arm. "But suppose there are some people who do like Mr. Scroggins and object to my taking down his posters?"

"Tell them," said the Senator, "tell them Scroggins himself told you to do it. That he is sending new posters with his name in bigger print. He is a vain coxcomb and it could well be true — it probably is true. I would put nothing by him."

"I'll do it," said Morgan James and started down the road.

"And one more thing," said the Senator. "Here are some sashes for the ladies — they go from the shoulder. Try to pick out the well-bosomed ones. It looks best on them. And one more thing. No torchlight parades. There are people in Studgeville who have torchlight parades. They almost cost me the election last time when they burnt down the town in a burst of enthusiasm."

"It's a pity we don't have the new Post Office yet," said Morgan James. "Made of stone like it is we could have the ladies in sashes with torches along the steps as you marched up or down, as the case might be."

"I can see you have a flair for politics, Morgan James."

"I think so," said Morgan James, "because I can see things like that so clearly."

"One more thing," said the Senator. "You may meet a man named Hamilton Roller. He is the head of the party in Studgeville, and he is very important to us and wants very much to be the first Postmaster of Studgeville."

"Do you think he will be a good Postmaster?"

"What has that got to do with it?" asked the Senator in astonishment. "One minute you amaze me with your vision of the steps of the new Post Office, and the next minute you ask me if Roller will be a good Postmaster. Now get on with you. I have to give solace to my poor widow lady and you have to get to work in Studgeville."

✿

Things went very well in Studgeville. Morgan James tore down every Scroggins poster until if you had asked a citizen of that community if they had ever heard of a Scroggins you would have received only the stare of a dead fish. The name of Bagful on the other hand was on the lips of everyone and especially on the bosoms of the most well endowed ladies. Little boys marched through town chanting "Bagful! Bagful! Bagful!" at the cost of ten cents a head. There were also groups of little girls who chanted as best they could. Morgan James charged them five cents a head for the privilege only because they wanted to so much. He hired one of those sandwich boards which fitted over the shoulders and the Temple of Minerva was paraded through Studgeville all evening except when the wearer was at the local Inn refreshing himself. In response to popular demand Morgan James bought a haystack on a hill on the edge of town and set fire to it just as the Senator came down the mountain into the square.

The evening was a great success. Morgan James was complimented by the Senator on his front work. He was invited to stand on the wagon with him when he spoke to the small multitude. The only hitch was the bands of little girls who kept chanting "Bagful! Bagful! Bagful!" It was fine at first but they wouldn't stop. Morgan James had to pay them ten cents a head to do so. He always suspected that they had heard of his arrangement with the boys.

The Senator was in good form. He started with the speech he had practiced on the stump, and then he moved on to the Post Office. "You have all seen," he said, "the picture of the new Post Office that is going to grace this Square after you have returned me as your Senator to Washington. You will notice the columns (all marble) and the steps (all marble) and the pedestal for the statue on top of the first Postmaster of the United States Studgeville Post Office. Modesty prevents him from standing forth at this time but" (and here the Senator looked down to his right at a short bristly redheaded man who took off his hat and bowed his head modestly) "but I think you all know to whom I refer!

"If ever I had any doubts as to the value and greatness of the U.S. Post Office, they were put to rest by my experience recently in our great Capital, and the compliment paid — if I may put it that way, and you will see in a moment why I put it that way — the compliment paid by the Regulars of his Britannic Majesty on their 'visit' to Washington when they burned that great white edifice we call our White House. They went first to what they considered to be the most important building in Washington, the hub of our communications, the very heart through which the lifeblood of our nation pulses — the U.S. Post Office. And they were repulsed. This young man and I" (the Senator put his arm around Morgan James' shoulder) "this young man and I repulsed a Company of British Regulars from the steps of the U.S. Post Office. It was only then that in rage and shame they went on to do their dastardly worst to our fair White House.

"But I am not here today nor are you here today to talk of the Washington Post Office. It is the new Studgeville Post Office that makes our hearts beat faster and brings pride to our cheeks. The world of Commerce will flourish. Our land will grow tenfold in value. The sun will rise and set on Studgeville time."

The Senator paused, but before the citizenry could cheer his speech, there were shouts from the rear of the crowd.

"Perry, Perry! Lake Erie!" And then chanting — "Perry, Perry, Perry!"

The Senator raised his arms for silence. "Ah, I see that some of my friends have heard my recounting of our great Victory last year on Lake Erie. And in response to popular demand I will share it with you again."

The Senator raised his arms again for complete silence. There was complete silence as he began: "The Americans go forward to meet the British, and in the inspired words of A. T. Tuckerman:

Sublime the pause, when down the gleaming tide
The virgin galleys to the conflict glide
The very wind as if in awe or grief
Scarce makes a ripple or disturbs a leaf.

The battle rages. Commodore Perry's ship is almost sunk and he must go to another." The Senator struck a pose with one leg forward as if standing in the prow of a skiff.

> A soul like his no danger fears;
> His pendant from the mast he tears,
> And in his gallant bosom bears
>   To grace the old Niagara.
> See!   He quits the Lawrence's side
> Where thundering navies round him ride.

"And the Battle rages on, back and forth, to and fro, until —

> As lifts the smoke what tongue can fitly tell
> The transports which those manly bosoms swell
> When Britain's ensign down the reeling mast
> Seeks to proclaim the desperate struggle past.

"And Commodore Perry writes his now immortal dispatch to the President — 'We have met the enemy, and they are ours: two ships, two brigs, one schooner, and one sloop.' "

There was silence for a moment and then cheers.

The Senator raised his hands again. "But the War is not over. General Jackson now stands before New Orleans awaiting a British Invasion. Many of our men are there with him today, and I know that all our hearts are with them. And I would hope that next year at this time I could come before you to celebrate Jackson's Victory at New Orleans as we have just celebrated Perry's at Lake Erie. Thank you."

3.

"You were in high form, Bagful," said Hamilton Roller the next morning at the Inn.

"I thank you," said the Senator. "Praise from you is praise indeed. And I think we have found in this gentleman the front man we all look for."

Morgan James felt himself blush, but he also felt the cold appraising look of Hamilton Roller.

"It's what I want to talk to you about, Bagful. Last night's performance won't wash in Seldom Seen."

"It won't?" said the Senator in disappointment. "I thought we might just handle it the same way."

"It won't wash, Bagful," repeated Roller. He looked at the Senator and then nodded in the direction of Morgan James. "But I have an idea how we might skin the cat."

"I think you had better leave us alone, Morgan James," said the Senator. "Mr. Roller has something to say in confidence."

Morgan James went out and stood on the porch of the Inn and surveyed the place of his triumph. When the little girls saw him they began to giggle and chant "Bagful! Bagful! Bagful!" It was a pity that in this moment of triumph Hamilton Roller should cast such a sour note over everything. Morgan James did not like him. He didn't like his red bristly hair, or his tummy captured like a little balloon by his belt, or his piggy eyes. He did not think that he would look well on the Temple of Minerva.

"Well, my boy," said the Senator, booming out behind him. "I think we have skinned the cat, as a matter of fact we have skinned two cats. A preacher went by here the other day on his way to Seldom Seen — God knows they need one."

"An un-Christian people no doubt," said Morgan James.

The Senator outlined the skinning of the cat. Morgan James would be in black frock coat and tall hat and white gloves. He would take the buggy himself to Seldom Seen. The Senator would follow. Morgan James would distribute the picture of the Temple of Minerva liberally about town. The Senator had never been to Seldom Seen and he understood it wasn't much, and therefore it might be worthwhile if Morgan James could be seen going about town making a survey of the buildings. If asked why, he would only say that Washington wanted it, that he didn't know why but it might be for taxes. He could do the same thing, in a way, about guns — just let it be known that he was taking a census of the number of firearms in Seldom Seen and again that he didn't know why it was something Washington wanted. Under no circumstances was he to enter one of the many saloons in town.

"No sashes?" said Morgan James.

"No sashes, no chanting, no bonfires! No hoopla all the way," said the Senator.

There was no doubt that Morgan James looked handsome in the black frock coat and tall hat and white gloves. The Senator had a cane for him too.

"No, I just want to see you walk back and forth. Sashay a little bit to show you're from Washington and want to show these country bumpkins how a real gentleman walks."

"I don't think I'm about to do that."

"You don't have to," said the Senator, "it was just an idea."

"I'm going to take my deerskin and the tassels with me, just in case."

"Now one more thing," said the Senator, after Morgan James was seated grandly in the buggy. "I don't want you to get in any altercations in Seldom Seen. They are a cantankerous people and you are apt to be provoked."

"I will turn my cheek," said Morgan James, putting

on his gloves and his hat, which was a little small and sat on his head like a stovepipe.

"And one more thing, it might be better not to mention my name. I'm not so sure how those scum of Seldom Seen view me."

"The name of Bagful will not cross my lips," said Morgan James and started up the horse. He felt very grand. He sat up straight. He wished that Annabel Lee could see him now. It must be how she felt when she stood at the tops of stairs.

It was a lovely day to travel the road along split-rail fences and apple trees. Every time he met someone he tipped his cane to his hat and nodded properly. There were few buildings now and what there were were not much — small log cabins without windows and scraggly shingled roofs and scraggly barefoot children and scraggly dogs. It was definitely not promising biscuit country. The road became steep and washed out. It was not really made for buggies. He was beginning to see why this town was called Seldom Seen. Then from the top of the hill he could see what there was of the town. It was only a cluster of houses on either side of the road. There was no church or if there was a church there was no steeple on it. The road running through town seemed to be full of dogs and pigs.

He had just started down the hill when there was a great *WHAM!* and his hat blew off. He picked it up and looked. . . . It had been shot straight through near the top. He rubbed his head. It seemed to be all right.

He looked back. A little brown-legged barefoot girl was coming down out of the rocks above the road with a rifle at least twice as long as she was high.

"You might of seriously injured me," said Morgan James. "Look where those holes are!"

"I just figured that unless you had an awful pointy head there wasn't going to be any head up there."

"You should have asked me first anyway. What's your name?"

"Abelia, A-B-E-L-I-A. If I hadn't shot that hat off somebody else would have and some of them don't shoot as well as me. An awful lot of people have been killed around here when they got their hats like that shot off with their heads inside."

"I guess I should say thank you!" said Morgan James.

"I think you should. I probably saved your life. You wouldn't have lasted two minutes in Seldom Seen with a hat like that. And you're not going to last one minute with those gloves and cane and frock coat. You look like a popinjay."

"I thought I looked pretty good," said Morgan James. "It's meant to be how they look in Washington."

"Washington!" said Abelia. "I don't know where it is, but it's a bad word around here. My father said he would cut off the privities of the first man that comes around here from Washington. You got any other clothes?"

"I have my deerskin jacket and deerskin pants all with deerskin tassels."

"I'll sit in the buggy and you can put 'em on."

"Your father said that?"

"He probably didn't really mean it, except he wasn't drunk when he said it."

"I'll put them on," said Morgan James, "except it's contrary to what the Senator said."

When he got back in the buggy he found Abelia's rifle sticking in his stomach. "Does everyone around here carry a rifle?"

"Everyone," said Abelia, and she thought a moment, "except children and they throw rocks."

"And how old are you?"

"I'm ten. My father says I never was a child. That's because I don't cry when he beats me."

"And why do you think that is?" said Morgan James.

"I think it's because he cries all the time when he gets drunk."

Morgan James thought Abelia was going to go on but she didn't, and if she wasn't going to Morgan James wasn't going to.

They were about halfway to town when Abelia said, "This is where I get out." She jumped off the buggy, took her rifle, went down a path through a thicket and disappeared. Morgan James hollered after her, "Good-bye!" There was no answer. Then he hollered again. "Thank you!" There was no answer to that either.

He started down the hill to town again without much enthusiasm. He could see that it wasn't going to be a lark like Studgeville. He couldn't understand why the

Senator had had him get dressed up the way he did. He had never felt comfortable. He was glad he had changed. He knew that Roller was behind it. But he would go ahead with the posters. He didn't need to do anything about the guns. He already knew the answer to that. Everyone in Seldom Seen carried a gun except the children and they threw rocks. He hoped that Annabel Lee would appreciate what he was going through for her. He would find a preacher in Seldom Seen and take him back to her and tears would come to her eyes and she would take her apron down from the hook and he would be home.

Seldom Seen was not much, in fact it was nothing. It was a mud hole. The chickens had to fly to get across the street. Only the pigs seemed to be happy. There were no women. The men were tall and mean and hungry-looking and slouched through the mud indifferently. They carried their rifles as if they were part of each other. Morgan James shuddered to think how they would have looked at him if he had not changed his clothes, or what they might have proposed to do to him.

He found a nice tree suitable for a poster. He stood on a rock to stick it up high and he was doing so when *WHAM*, and suddenly there was a large hole where Minerva had been standing on top of her temple. The shot must have gone over his head and between his arms. He hardly dared to turn around. He didn't want to aggravate any of those men.

51

But it was Abelia. "Somebody was going to do it," she said, "and better me."

Morgan James was still trembling. "I'm sure you're right," he said, "but still you should have told me you were going to do it."

"It wouldn't be any fun that way. I wanted it to be a su-prise." Abelia led the way to a falling-down wagon. "I brought you something to eat. You look pale. We better sit up here or the pigs will get it. I hate pigs, don't you?"

"I couldn't agree more," said Morgan James. He was hungry. It was a biscuit with ham and green-like onions. He took a bite. His mouth was on fire. He could feel smoke coming out of his nose and ears. He could barely see Abelia through his watering eyes.

He breathed out until there was nothing left to breathe out. "Wh — Wh — What?" he said.

Abelia was happily munching away. "Ramps," she said.

Morgan James ran to a spring to get some water. He considered putting his whole head in the spring. "Oh," he said, "I never tasted anything like that."

"Some people think they're too hot," said Abelia. "I like 'em."

"I've heard of them," said Morgan James, "and I heard they were hot, but not like this."

"Ramps are ramps," said Abelia. "There's a whole lot near those rocks where I saw you this morning. But don't tell anybody. People around here go crazy for ramps in the Spring."

"Not a word," said Morgan James. He was still hungry but the hunger, no matter how great, did not include ramps.

Abelia took his biscuit. "I'll take the ramps and you take the rest."

"Have you seen a preacher? I heard there was a preacher coming."

"He's up at the funeral."

"Maybe I'll go up there," said Morgan James. "I have to find a preacher."

"I wouldn't go up there."

"I have to find him," said Morgan James.

"It's a Trible funeral," said Abelia. "There's always shooting at a Trible funeral."

"I hope they don't shoot the preacher, because I need him to marry me."

"It's a mistake," said Abelia. "There's nobody happy after they get married. I would like to get that preacher to baptize me. I've been wanting that for a long time."

"I don't know if I've been baptized or not."

"You'd know," said Abelia. "You get your name soaked into you like dyeing wool. The way it is now sometimes I wonder if I'm Abelia or not."

"I've always been pretty attached to my name and vice versa."

"You've been baptized then," said Abelia. She

jumped down from the wagon. "You going to put up more posters?"

"I am," said Morgan James. "This is the Temple of Minerva, you know. It's what the new Post Office is going to look like."

"In Seldom Seen?"

"Or Studgeville. One or t'other."

"That'll be the day."

They came to a tree that already had a poster on it calling for brave volunteers from Tennessee to join General Andrew Jackson in New Orleans to fight the British.

"I think I might go," said Abelia.

"You can't go," said Morgan James, "you're a girl, but I think after I get married I might go."

"Maybe you want to have a shoot-out with me to see who goes."

"Look," said Morgan James, "at all those people coming down the mountain."

In the lead was a black hearse with black horses with tall tassels on their heads. On each corner of the hearse was a brass lantern that flickered in the falling light. Then behind there were rows of horsemen in twos with guns across their laps and their hats pulled low over their heads. They came slowly into town. The hearse went on and the men tied up at the saloon.

"It's the Tribles from the funeral," said Abelia.

"They don't look very happy."

"It's probably because they didn't find anybody for to shoot at the funeral."

"Look now at those two men coming out on the porch of the saloon."

"Never saw them before," said Abelia. "They're not from Seldom Seen."

Morgan James had to look twice, but there was no doubt, it was Hamilton Roller and the Senator. They looked like they must have rolled all the way from Studgeville. Their hats were crushed. Their clothes were old and torn. They needed shaves. They both carried guns. Roller pointed his gun to the sky and fired. There was a rush of men from the bar.

The Senator raised his arms. Roller called for silence. The Senator looked around. "I'm just goin' to take a moment of your time, boys, and then we're goin' in for a drink or two or three, on me—Bagful." Somebody fired from one end of the street. Somebody else fired from the other end. The Senator held up his arms again for silence. "I'm a poor man, as you can see, but I've got enough to share with my friends in Seldom Seen. Now, boys, like it or not, there's goin' to be an election and somebody's got to go to Washington to be Senator from Tennessee. Now if any of you boys want to go to Washington, step right up." He paused and looked around. No one stepped up. If anything, the crowd shrank away from him. "Now what I'm concerned about, boys, is not the going to Washington. If I have to go, and you want me to go, I'll go, but what I've got on my mind is seeing that Washington don't come here to Seldom Seen. Because if you give 'em a chance they'll come. Oh Lord, will they come, wagonloads of 'em, with forms to fill out. They'll be here. They've been here." Somebody in the crowd cried "Where?" and fired off a gun. The Senator held up his hands. "Scroggins. Does that name ring a bell? Scroggins has been here. He has had his man from Washington here. I don't see him now — a young man in fancy dress with gloves and cane. A popinjay from Washington."

"That's you," said Abelia, "and that was my father who fired the last time. You better get out of here."

"Me?" said Morgan James, "I was just meant to be pretending I was from Washington."

"You're going to be a dead pretender in two minutes," said Abelia and ran down a side street. "Come on!"

"I know that popinjay has been here," shouted the Senator. "I've seen those posters he put up, and you know what they are, that's the Temple of Meenervah that's going to be the new Post Office in Seldom Seen — and you know who's going to pay for it? You — and you — and you." The shooting became general.

Morgan James knew it was time to get out of there. This wasn't pretending anymore. He ran to where Abelia was calling him.

He heard Hamilton Roller shout, "I see him, there he goes, boys, get him!"

Abelia led the way around a barn. Morgan James could hear the crowd whooping and hollering as it came down Main Street. Everybody seemed to be firing now. "This way," said Abelia. She ran up to where the hearse was standing and opened the back door and pushed Morgan James inside. There was a thing like a stretcher there and she made him lie down and she covered him with a sheet. Then she went out the other end.

Morgan James heard somebody shout, "Where'd he go? Where'd he go?"

"Into those woods," said Abelia. "He skedaddled over that fence into the woods. I saw him just like that."

"After him, boys!" someone shouted, and then there was more shooting.

"I'm going to look in here," somebody said and opened the door to the hearse. "Just some stiff," he said and closed the door.

Morgan James lay there very quietly for a long time where so many bodies had lain. It was very strange. One thing you couldn't imagine was how you would feel if you were dead, because you wouldn't feel, would you, and how could you imagine not feeling? It was enough to make him very sleepy, which it did. Sometime later, after all the shouting and shooting had calmed down, he reviewed the behavior of Roller, the Senator, and Abelia. Abelia was a genuine heroine. The Senator was a miserable man who knew better. Roller didn't know better and was a skunk. Morgan James felt in control — having made those very definite classifications — and he went to sleep.

He had no idea what time it was when he felt the wagon jolt to a start. He lay absolutely still until he was sure that they were out of town. There seemed to be some horsemen riding alongside. There were two very small windows on the back of the van. Morgan James peeked out. There was a horseman on each side riding easily along with a rifle across the lap. There were two men up front in the seat of the van, which was separated from him by a curtain. The man on the right, who sat very tall in his seat with the tall black hat, must be the preacher. The man on the left was quite small. He was leaning forward toward the horses with the reins in his lap.

Morgan James waited a little bit and then tapped the man on the right very lightly on the shoulder. "Sh — sh," he whispered.

The man never turned around. He looked even straighter ahead.

"Whitemason," he said very quietly, "that Trible boy has returned."

"Nonsense, Drummond, that Trible boy was put away as permanently as any I've ever seen."

"Then maybe one of the others who has ridden in

this van has come back. There must have been hundreds to whom you have given their last ride."

"Thousands, I'm sure, but I always make certain that they're gone before that dirt goes on. When I was young I had one sit up in the grave. He was half covered with dirt, and he sat up and yelled, 'What the Hell is going on?' It gave me a start I can tell you, Drummond, but it also taught me the power of a Rising."

"We know about that, Reverend."

"Do we not, Drummond, do we not."

So the little man on the left was the Reverend Whitemason and the other man was called Drummond. He must travel with the Preacher. He had a real English accent. He certainly wasn't from Seldom Seen.

This time Morgan James tapped the Preacher on the shoulder and whispered, "Sh — sh — sh."

"What is it, Drummond?" said the Preacher.

"What is what?"

"You tapped me on the shoulder and said 'Sh — sh.' "

The man called Drummond was annoyed. "I did not tap you on the shoulder. Nor did I say 'Sh — sh!' "

"Then somebody did," said the Preacher. "Take a look."

"I will not take a look," said Drummond. "I will leave this conveyance before I take a look."

"Then I will stop the van and we will both take a look. It is probably only some poor inebriated soul who has crawled in there for some peace and quiet."

The last thing that Morgan James wanted was for the van to stop with those two horsemen riding alongside waiting to shoot somebody. Maybe Roller had sent them out to look for him. He put his head almost between them. "It's me, Morgan James," he said. "I'm hiding."

Drummond put his hand on Morgan James' head. "It's a very solid head," he said. He looked at him. "You're the young man from Washington the Senator denounced."

"Who are those men riding alongside?" said Morgan James.

"Two of the Trible boys, giving us safe passage," said Drummond.

"We were threatened with bodily loss of life and limb by some of the enemies of the Trible family," said the Preacher.

Morgan James felt more secure. He could not have imagined better protection than the Trible boys. "What in the world could anyone have against the Trible boys?"

"There was some feeling among some that the Trible boy should not be buried with the benefit of clergy," said Drummond.

"Very narrow-minded," said Morgan James. He felt very well. The cool night air was sweet. The horses were moving smoothly. The Trible boys jogged easily alongside and then pulled ahead to go darkly down the road together knee to knee. He wondered how Annabel Lee was. She was probably just sleeping, dreaming sweet dreams of him no doubt. He could smell the biscuits in her hair. His mouth was watering. He would tell her someday that when he thought of her it made his mouth water. He had learned that it was important to Annabel Lee for her to be told how he felt about her, and something like this would make her very happy. It would probably bring tears to her sweet eyes that his deepest thoughts of her were so powerful it made his mouth water.

"What's that noise?" said Drummond nervously.

"It's my stomach," said Morgan James.

"And you have been eating ramps, sir," said Drummond.

They came out suddenly from under the trees into a white patch of moonlight. Morgan James could get a good look at Drummond. He could see that he was very tall and thin, gaunt, with a long-lived face. "Do you like ramps?" said Morgan James.

"I regret to say that I am addicted. Nothing like them in England. Nothing like them probably on this whole globe, but they should be eaten in togetherness. If you are suddenly overwhelmed with a desire to partake, be a man, and announce to your comrades, 'I am going to eat a ramp,' and then they may go and do likewise."

The two Trible boys had stopped on a small knoll ahead of them. The Preacher pulled up his van when he came to them. Morgan James ducked back behind the curtain so they wouldn't see him. He couldn't hear what they said but he heard the Preacher say that he was much obliged.

"They're going back," said the Preacher. "They say we'll be all right now. They say they'll be coming back this way soon with the volunteers for Jackson's army."

"Where are we going now?" asked Morgan James as they started up.

"Right now," said the Preacher, "we're going down this hill where the Trible boys say is a good place to stop, and then I have many duties and then Memphis."

"Someplace in there you're going to have to marry me."

"I tell you what," said the Preacher. "You can make yourself useful at the baptisms and the burials and the weddings along with Peter Drummond, and then we'll get you married. Where does this fair maid live?"

"Sort of north of Studgeville."

"That will work out very well," said the Preacher. "In about a month or so. I have neglected that part of the country."

Morgan James slept peacefully that night under the van. Nobody was chasing him. Nobody was shooting over his shoulder. Life almost immediately settled into a very pleasant routine. They had plenty to eat. The

Preacher was usually paid in eggs and biscuits, ham and venison, and vegetables of all kinds.

All along the road there were people waiting for them. It had been a long time since the Preacher had been through. There were graves with limestones at the head and feet to be prayed over. There were marriages that hadn't waited with children at the side. And they baptized them. Morgan James liked the baptizing the best. Many of the girls were full-grown, it had been so long since the Preacher had been through. They came in short white shifts. Peter Drummond and Morgan James were stationed in the water. Peter Drummond on one side. Morgan James on the other.

The girl came shivering down into the water. The Preacher stood on the bank. He always seemed to stutter at this moment.

"And now in the n-n-name of the Lord, D-D-Dunk her! I christen thee M-me-hitabel."

Peter Drummond and Morgan James would dunk her. Sometimes the loose shift would go up at first under the chin of the baptizee, but they would push her all the way under, head and all. Afterward she would come out with the white gown stuck tight to her now pure body. It was to Morgan James a wonderful sample of the wondrous ways of the Lord.

As they got nearer to Memphis the roads became filled with volunteers slouching with their long rifles on their way to join Andrew Jackson. Everybody said that there was going to be a big battle with the British at New Orleans depending on when everybody got there. It hurt Morgan James to think that he might miss it, but he had promised Annabel Lee about the preacher and he was going to do it.

One day he and Peter Drummond were sitting by the side of the road on a hill watching some of the Kentucky men. They were big men. They seemed to glide along like Indians, putting their feet down flat in front of them. A lot of them wore their boots tied over their shoulders.

Suddenly there was a *WHAM* and Peter Drummond's tall black hat blew off.

"Oh, no," said Morgan James.

There was a cheer from the Kentuckians.

"My word," said Peter Drummond.

A small, a tiny figure left the line on the road and came toward them. The rifle was longer than the person was high.

"Abelia!" said Morgan James. "I thought I told you to let folks know when you were about to do that."

She held up a finger to her lips. "They think I'm a boy. I call myself James Morgan now."

Peter Drummond was sticking a finger through the hole in his hat.

"Guess I didn't hurt you, did I?" she said. "I thought you must be a friend of Morgan James or I wouldn't have done it."

"I understand completely, James Morgan," said Peter Drummond. "So you're going to New Orleans with the Kentucky people?"

"Kentucky sharpshooters is what we are. Probably the best you know."

"I didn't thank you for what you did for me in Seldom Seen, Abelia." Morgan James turned to Peter Drummond. "She saved my life, you know. That Senator was threatening me."

"A bufflehead," said Peter Drummond. "A true bufflehead."

"Amen," said Abelia.

Abelia stayed with them a couple of days while the Kentucky sharpshooters camped down the road. Peter Drummond took a great shine to her, which was strange because he was a Lord, or at least his father was — who sent him a check every month, or at least did until the oldest brother became Duke and he didn't. But as the Preacher said, Peter Drummond was a true gentleman except when he succumbed to spirits. At night he read *Pilgrim's Progress* to her, which she liked very much.

One night they came to the Slough of Despond.

"Where does it say that?" she said.

"Here," said Peter Drummond.

"S-L-O-U-G-H, that's 'sl-oww.' That's the way my grandmother read it when she was alive."

"You're right," said Peter Drummond, and afterward he always read it as "sl-oww."

"Have you ever been in there — in the Slough of Despond?" asked Abelia.

"I've been there," said Peter Drummond.

"Me, too," said Abelia. "I like Great-Heart the best, don't you?"

The time was getting close for her to go off with the Kentuckians. It was already fall. Peter Drummond had promised that she would be baptized. The Preacher was hesitant about this girl who went around like a boy, but Peter Drummond persuaded him, and persuaded him, too, that it would be a very private affair so that no one else would know the true state of affairs. He insisted that day that Abelia go down to the river and bathe and wash her hair and everything. She resisted but Peter Drummond was firm. He found a clean white shirt of his for her to wear. It came down to her ankles, but he combed her hair and put a ribbon in it. It turned her very shy and she twirled around once for them all to see.

The four of them went down to the river. Peter Drummond sang —

Let us gather by the Ri-ver
The beautiful, beautiful Ri-ver.

And they dunked her. She came up like a wet water rat. She was shivering. "D-d-do it again."

"I don't think . . . ," said the Preacher.

Peter Drummond nodded at him fiercely. "The

whole thing?" he said to Abelia. "Th-th- whole th-thing," said Abelia, still shivering.

Peter Drummond sang —

Let us gather by the Ri-ver
The beautiful, beautiful Ri-ver.

The Preacher began again, "And now in the n-n-name of the Lord, D-D-Dunk her! I christen thee Abelia."

4.

Peter Drummond went into the Slough of Despond when Abelia left. He moped around. It took him a minute or two to answer a question, as if he had to come back from a long way away. He went on long walks alone and never said where he had been. He didn't even bother to put the ramps which Morgan James gathered for him into his scrambled eggs.

The Preacher was very upset. "I am worried," he said one day to Morgan James, "about our friend Peter Drummond. This is the way he acts just before he has one of his spells." The Preacher was very fond of Peter Drummond, but he never showed it really. He was a small man like one of those small birds you see whizzing through the sky going someplace as straight and fast as they can. The Preacher was saving Souls, but he didn't really see them. Peter Drummond had been in the Slough of Despond a long time before the

Preacher had noticed it. And it disquieted him. It distracted him from his fast straight line. But he didn't preach at him. He just looked at Peter Drummond with sad, not understanding eyes.

"I can see," he said once to Morgan James, "that the Lord is leading us to a Rising."

Morgan James did not question. The Preacher often talked in Capital Letters like that — Risings, and Fallings, Lust and Avarice, Modesty and Chastity. He did it so naturally that Morgan James was sure that he probably even talked to himself in Capital Letters. Morgan James started to do it himself, like when he thought how much he wanted to see Annabel Lee, who was another One who was on a Straight Track. There seemed to be all these People who were on Straight Tracks, like Dr. Coffin and the Senator and the Preacher. Peter Drummond was different, just as he himself was different. Morgan James had always been happy just going along. But now, of course, he found himself on Annabel Lee's Track leading to Marriage and it had complicated his Life to where he was run out of towns he had never been run out of before and had holes shot in his hat. It was not all good, but a Life without Annabel Lee was too Awful to contemplate.

They were camped at this time at a fairgrounds outside of the town of Crab Bottom. Crab Bottom was one of the fastest-growing towns in the area, so fast in fact that it had become very civic-minded, and the most civic-minded people in Crab Bottom were on the move to change the name to Fair View as one more appealing to new business. The Fair was the big event of the Spring. There were two-legged races and three-legged races. There were sheep-shearing contests. There were quilt displays. There were dog trials and target shooting and rail splitting. And at night there was a Revival where people had Visions and Came Forward and some wrapped rattlesnakes about themselves. There was something for everybody. And on one night the Preacher was to have his service.

In the afternoons they "dipped the sheep" as Peter Drummond called it. One day they baptized over one hundred and fifty, and the one-hundred-and-fifty-sixth got as full a treatment as the first. The Preacher insisted on it. One large fat girl went down like a whale and took Peter Drummond and Morgan James down with her. She like to drowned. There seemed to be nothing to grab hold of or nothing small enough to grab hold of. The crowd on the bank cheered and hooted. The Preacher stood patiently. Finally she got up by herself, wheezing and spouting, and flailing her arms so that she knocked Morgan James and Peter Drummond down again as they tried to get up.

But there was one event during the Fair that took Peter Drummond out of his despair and restored him. It was the arrival from New Orleans of a balloon with two Frenchmen.

Morgan James saw it first. They were eating lunch at

the van. It was a huge round ball in the sky with a basket hanging below it. He could not believe it. He could only point up.

The Preacher took off his glasses and examined them.

"Ah," said Peter Drummond, "it is a *ballon*."

"A what?" said Morgan James.

"It's French. I saw one of the first in Paris about twenty years ago. They call it a *ballon. On — on —* like a pig!"

"How do you say that? Balloon?"

"If you want. They put gas inside. The gas is lighter than air so it goes up."

"I never," said the Preacher.

"Me neither," said Morgan James, but he was going to go up in one. He had to. The men in the basket were waving.

Peter Drummond shouted to them in French.

They waved even more wildly.

Since Peter Drummond was the only man in Crab Bottom who spoke French they saw a lot of the two Frenchmen from the balloon. They were a pair. One was short and fat and waved his arms and talked all the time very fast. The other was small and thin and waved his arms and talked all the time very fast. They both thought they could talk English. They came out every night to the van for supper with a bottle of wine. They thought ramps were wonderful. They carried on with cries of wonder before they ate them, waved their arms while they did eat them, and sent kisses to the sky and thanks to the Lord after they did eat them.

They said they were on their way to Washington, but they promised Peter Drummond and Morgan James a ride before they left. The Preacher declined. He did not altogether approve of them, but, on the other hand, he was pleased that they proved his long-held view that the French were an Unstable, Dangerous people under the Yoke of the Scarlet Lady of Rome.

Someone had to help the Preacher that day set up benches in the tent for his service and it was agreed that Peter Drummond would go up first since he could talk French. Morgan James watched them attach this barrel of gas to the bag and the bag got bigger and bigger until it started to rise and pull at the ropes. Then the ropes which attached it to the ground were loosed and it rose slowly and gently. It didn't seem that remarkable when you saw it happening, but it was definitely something that Morgan James was going to do. They promised that they would not go far, and at first they went up pretty straight. Peter Drummond was shouting and waving. He had a wine bottle in his hand which Morgan James was not happy to see, but he was happy to see that Peter Drummond had come out of the Slough of Despond.

Then a wind came up and they sailed off, taking the flag of France high over Tennessee. Morgan James spent the afternoon setting up benches in the big tent for the Revival. It was the big event of the Fair. It was guessed that maybe a hundred people would Come Forward. And a Mountain Man was going to be there who let rattlesnakes bite him. And some people were going to talk in Voices. There was going to be a Laying On of Hands to cure the sick. And there was a dulcimer and fiddle player for the songs and hymns.

Some of this, like the snakes and the talking in Voices, the Preacher did not approve of, but as he said to Morgan James, "Sometimes the Lord needs help, and if it gets them in the Tent and they hear some good Gospel it is all to the good. But I would dearly Love to have a Sign."

"Maybe we could put one on the balloon when I go up in it and then everybody could see it," said Morgan James.

"A Sign, Morgan James, a Sign to these Dissolute People to mend their ways."

"Of course," said Morgan James.

He kept looking around all day for the balloon. There was no sign of it. It was getting very late and he was getting very nervous.

The tent had already started to fill up when the balloonists returned. They were in a wagon. Peter Drummond was stretched out in the back of the wagon.

"Je suis désolé," said the fat Frenchman.

"I am sad," said the thin Frenchman.

73

Morgan James went to help Peter Drummond out of the wagon. His hands were ice cold. He seemed stiff.

"Il est mort," said the fat Frenchman.

"He is dead," said the thin Frenchman.

"But how?" said Morgan James.

They shrugged and made motions of drinking out of a bottle and then both collapsed in a heap on the ground.

"It is a Sign," said the Preacher. "I knew we would have a Sign. And now we will have a Rising. He will Rise and All will see the Wonder of it."

"But he's dead," said Morgan James. "Feel his hands."

"No matter," said the Preacher, "it was done once before with Peter Drummond and it shall be done again. It was in the town of Fast Branch and he was like this and he came up. The plate was passed and I spoke the Word over him and he Rose. Almost a hundred dollars the Lord took in that night. Bring him to the back of the Tent."

The Frenchmen were beginning to get the idea.

"Il est fou," said the fat Frenchman of the Preacher.

"He is crazy," said the thin Frenchman.

They both made the sign for "crazy" with their fingers pointing to their heads.

Morgan James felt so badly for Peter Drummond. He knew it was Abelia's leaving that had done it. He had not been able to accept that.

The Preacher refused to come in the tent for the first

74

part of the Revival, but the Frenchmen and Morgan James watched the Mountain Man.

He was called the Mountain Man because he came from the mountains and was built like a mountain. Even the big rattlesnakes did not look that big when they wrapped around him. Then he put his wrist right in a rattlesnake's mouth and let him bite. Several people fainted and the Frenchmen cried how marvelous it was and kissed each other.

Then there was the Talking-in-Voices, when people just got up and talked what sounded like nonsense to Morgan James with made-up words from long-ago lost languages. Even the Frenchmen got up and talked French and were a great success. One of them talked in glowing terms of something called "filet de sole" which sounded very very religious and the other talked of "croissants" which clearly had to do with crosses.

Then everyone sang "Church in the Dell."

Come, Come, Come, Come, Come, Come, Come,
To the Church in the Wild Wood.

Come, Come, Come, Come, Come, Come, Come,
To the Church in the Vale.

Morgan James had never been able to get it straight how many "comes" there were. He usually did too many once he got started.

It was time for the Preacher to play his part. He

explained to Morgan James how it would go. The Frenchmen would wheel Peter Drummond in under a sheet on a cart. The Preacher would Preach. Then the sheet would be taken off. Morgan James would pass a plate for the money. Then Morgan James would kneel by the body and the Preacher would Preach over it.

"And when I say 'Rise, Peter Drummond,' you will bite his hand."

"Bite his hand?" said Morgan James.

"You will bite his hand," said the Preacher. "It is just a small thing to help the Lord to his Purpose."

"Impossible," said Morgan James. Just the idea sent shivers through him.

"Do you wish the Lord to take you and Annabel Lee into a State of Connubial Bliss?"

"I do," said Morgan James, "you know I do, but this is too much. Maybe one of the Frenchmen could do it. They're sort of crazy."

"They are not of our Faith, Morgan James. You are the one to do it. For the sake of the Lord and for Peter Drummond. And when I say 'Rise, Peter Drummond,' you will bite — for Annabel Lee, Morgan James."

"I'll do it," said Morgan James.

"Good," said the Preacher, "and one more thing. Here is a handkerchief."

Morgan James took it. "Good Lord!" he said. "I'm sorry, but it's full of ramp."

"It is," said the Preacher. "You may put it to your

76

eyes now and then to bring the tears, which will add a nice appearance, and at the moment I say 'Rise, Peter Drummond' and you bite his hand you will put this handkerchief to his mouth and nose. We must do every little thing to help the Lord to His Purpose."

It went pretty much like the Preacher said. He preached. Then the Frenchmen wheeled Peter Drummond in on a cart. They took the sheet off. Then they sang:

> *Let us gather by the Ri-ver!*
> *The beautiful, beautiful Ri-ver!*

It made Morgan James sad to sing when he remembered how beautifully Peter Drummond had sung the day of Abelia's baptism.

Several people came up to Peter Drummond and put their hands on him. Then they would nod as if in agreement.

Then Morgan James went up and knelt at the cart. The thin Frenchman passed the plate. The Preacher looked out over the crowd. There was perfect silence. Then he looked at the sky. Then he looked at Morgan James, who put the handkerchief to his eyes. There were shivers going up and down Morgan James' back, but he took Peter Drummond's cold, cold hand and put it to his lips.

"Rise, Peter Drummond!" the Preacher said. Morgan James closed his eyes and took a nip of the hand. Just a little nip. He opened his eyes. Peter Drummond was still, still, still.

"*Rise*, Peter Drummond, *Rise!*" said the Preacher. A woman shrieked and keeled over. Morgan James took a real nip this time. He put the handkerchief to Peter Drummond's face. He put the handkerchief to his own face and it did revive him. He looked up at the Preacher. "I say unto all of you for Peter Drummond shall *RISE*. Do not *BITE* the hand that feeds you. Let Peter Drummond *RISE!*" Morgan James really bit a finger this time. He squeezed the handkerchief until the ramp juice was running down Peter Drummond's chin. There was no Life. There was silence.

The Frenchmen stepped in and pulled the sheet up and wheeled Peter Drummond away. The Preacher just stood there. He could not believe it. Morgan James had to lead him out of the tent. From outside he could hear some angry rumblings of disappointed people. He was glad this wasn't Seldom Seen, where there certainly would have been shooting.

But the crowd did leave. The Frenchmen were very nervous. Morgan James had never seen such shrugging. He thought their eyes might roll out. The Preacher just sat with his head down. He did not move. It was as if he had been dropped from a great height *PLOPLOP* into the Slough of Despond.

They were like that for a long time when they heard

78

it. It was a dull roar and a glow of light coming out of the town. It was a crowd — an angry crowd — led by the Mountain Man.

"It will be — how do you say? — a feathering!" said one of the Frenchmen. "Bitume."

"Les oiseaux," said the other and flapped his arms like a bird.

"Les plumes," said the first. "Le bitume et les plumes."

"Tar and feathers," said Morgan James. "We better get out of here."

They put Peter Drummond and the Preacher in the van. The Frenchmen and Morgan James jumped on and they took off. The fat Frenchman drove the cart the way he did everything else, fast and nervously, disregarding bumps and puddles and scaring the poor horses to death with whatever he was shouting at them in French. But it was what was needed at the moment. The Mountain Man was not to be fooled with.

Morgan James was wedged between the Frenchmen, which was just as well because they were going so fast over so many bumps that his bottom never touched the seat except occasionally.

"Where do we go?" he shouted at the driver.

"Le Ballon," shouted the driver.

"Le Ballon," shouted the second Frenchman.

And the horses went faster into the night.

Morgan James looked into the back of the van. The

Preacher was sitting cross-legged with Peter Drummond's head in his lap. He was making soft cooing noises like a child to his doll. His glasses had fallen off his nose. He was in a bad state.

They didn't dare show a light for fear it would be seen and because fire would set off the gas. They had only the little moonlight to put more gas in the balloon. They had to put a lot in because this time there would be so many of them going up — the two Frenchmen, the Preacher, Peter Drummond, and Morgan James.

But you could be sure that the Mountain Man and the others would be coming. The Frenchmen had made too much noise with the horses for it to be any mystery about where they had gone. But there was nothing to do except to sit and listen to the gas seep into the balloon which didn't seem to get bigger at all.

The Frenchmen were very subdued for them. They whispered to each other and shrugged quietly. It was too dark to see if their eyes were rolling but they probably were.

The clouds were clearing from the full moon and while it made the world light it also made for dark shadows which seemed to make the world double. It did not make Morgan James feel better.

The business of biting Peter Drummond's hand had taken a lot out of him. And then there had been the Mountain Man coming after them. First he had been chased out of Seldom Seen and now chased out of Crab Bottom. If he ever got back to Annabel Lee he

was not going to leave and he was never going to flee
again.

They had almost put enough gas in the balloon
when they heard the crowd coming. They were not
coming by the road but through the woods beyond the
field where the balloon was. The bag was not yet full.
It was not yet pulling at the ropes when the towns-
people came out of the woods. The Mountain Man was
in the lead. He had a big torch and you could see him
very clearly. You could see how big he was with a
black beard and a head that looked as though it had
snakes in it. They didn't run toward the balloon but
came slowly, spread out across the field with torches.

"Le feu et le gaz, *Ka-Boom!*" said the fat Frenchman.

"Fire and gas, *KA-BOOM!*" said the thin Frenchman.

But it was too late to run and they had hidden the
horses in the woods.

The bag was beginning to fill now. It was beginning
to pull at the ropes.

"En avant!" cried the Frenchmen. "En avant!"

They climbed into the basket, but it was going to
be too late. The Mountain Man was almost on them.

"We forgot Peter Drummond," cried Morgan James
and jumped out of the basket.

Peter Drummond was still stretched out on the
ground in his sheet.

WHEN — SUDDENLY he rose up with the sheet

about him. He looked around and spread his arms like a great white bird in the moonlight.

"I have Risen," he whooped and ran toward the Mountain Man, flapping his arms in his white sheet in the moonlight like a great bird about to take off. *"Whoop — Whoop!"* he cried.

The Mountain Man took one look and dropped his torch and ran. Everybody ran. Peter Drummond stood alone in the field whooping and turning round and round alone in the field with his wings outstretched.

The Frenchmen clapped and hugged each other and cried, "Merveilleux!"

They took off about dawn with the sun coming up orange through the fog. They rose slowly until they were above the mist. The tops of the mountains peeked through, white with frost, glistening in the new sun. The basket rocked and Morgan James did not feel so good. He knew it was a beautiful sight. But it didn't feel like a beautiful sight.

Peter Drummond was in high spirits. "The last thing I remember was I was up in the balloon and then I woke up under the sheet. And then that big man was being very threatening. Never saw him before in my life. I must have missed something."

"You did," said the Preacher sadly. His Faith had not been Restored.

Peter Drummond missed that. "But I say, I feel tip-top now. Except my hand hurts. Feels like something bit me."

"I did," said Morgan James. He did feel better knowing that that cold dead hand he had bitten had not been dead.

"Oh, I say. We had a Rising and you bit me. And I didn't Rise."

"Now you have it," said Morgan James.

Peter Drummond dropped to his knees beside the Preacher. "Oh, I say, Whitemason, I am sorry. I know how much a good Rising means to you. You mustn't take it personally. You did your best. It still worked. Just a delayed reaction. Come on now, old boy, on your feet. You can't see anything from the bottom of the basket." He brought the Preacher to his feet and leaned him against the edge of the basket. He put his glasses firmly on his nose.

It was no use. The Preacher could not see the steamy mist of frost rising from the mountains and each drop a changing prism of blues and greens.

"I say, Whitemason, have you ever seen such a Morning? And you can't give Thanks? What will HE say?"

The Preacher shook his head. "I am a poor wretch, Peter Drummond. I have cast myself out of the Fold."

"There it is, Morgan James," said Peter Drummond. "He has cast himself out of the Fold. Whitemason has cast Whitemason out of the Fold."

"You are right, Peter Drummond," said the Preacher after a moment. "The Lord has shared his wisdom with you."

"Say Thanks to the Morning, Whitemason," said Peter Drummond.

"I will do as you suggest, Peter Drummond." The Preacher looked about him. It was as if he saw the mist and the mountains and felt the gentle rocking of the basket for the first time. He took off his glasses and wiped them. There must have been mist on them. Everybody bowed their heads. "We thank Thee, oh Lord, for this Morning you have Given us." He looked at the Frenchmen to make sure that they understood they could also enjoy this Gift even though they were of a Suspect Faith and even though they didn't understand what he had said. "And may we Show in All Ways that we are Deserving of such Beneficence."

"Amen," said Peter Drummond.

"Amen," said Morgan James.

"Grâce à Dieu," whispered the Frenchmen.

"Look," said Morgan James. "I bet that's Studgeville." He could see the town square very clearly where the Senator had spoken and the well-bosomed ladies had paraded with their sashes across their bosoms. It seemed like such a long time ago, but it was Studgeville all right. They were quite low over the town. They could see the people looking up. Some waved at first. Some took one look and ran into the church. Someone rang the bell. In a moment the whole square

84

was empty. If it was Studgeville Annabel Lee could not be far away. Wouldn't she be surprised and her mother, too, when he showed up in a balloon and with a Preacher too?

They cleared the mountain above Studgeville. Morgan James could see clearly at the top of the mountain where the Senator had practiced his speech. They were moving very fast. Coming over the mountain they were caught in the downdraft and taken down. It was a sinking feeling. Even the breakfast he hadn't eaten started to move up in his stomach. "Ooh la la!" cried the Frenchmen. Even that veteran balloonist Peter Drummond looked pale. The Preacher seemed almost pleased that the Laws of Nature were finally catching up with this balloon, which should never have gone up in the first place.

"There," said Morgan James. "Down there!" It was Annabel Lee's mother out with a gun. Annabel Lee had a broom.

They were low now and dropping fast. Annabel Lee's mother pointed the gun at them. "Mais non!" shouted the fat Frenchman. "*Ka-Boom!*" shouted the thin Frenchman.

"No, it's me, Morgan James. I have returned!" He leaned way over the edge of the basket. He couldn't hear what they shouted but Annabel Lee's mother dropped the gun and Annabel Lee waved the broom. "This is where I get off," said Morgan James.

It was almost an unnecessary remark. He had been

85

leaning way over the edge of the basket to shout. There was a lurch of wind. And then a crash. Morgan James went out. He fell. All he could think was that it was such an unfortunate thing to have happened at the last moment. It happened so fast that he couldn't even close his eyes or hold his breath. He kept waiting to hear himself hit the ground and bounce maybe. Maybe just a little bounce and then the End.

There was no bounce. It was water and mud. It was the beaver pond. He stood up with the water and mud to his waist. He thought he felt all right. He could see Annabel Lee and her mother running toward him.

"Well, I never," said Annabel Lee's mother.

"And what do you think you're doing in there, Morgan James?" said Annabel Lee.

"I don't know what it is he has about that beaver pond," said Annabel Lee's mother.

"He's come home, Momma," said Annabel Lee.

"If pigs could fly!" said her mother.

Morgan James struggled to the shore. Annabel Lee threw herself into his muddy arms.

"You'll get yourself all mud, Annabel Lee," said her mother. But she did come up, lean over, and kiss Morgan James on the cheek.

"I don't care," said Annabel Lee. "He's my hero."

"And I brought you a preacher," said Morgan James. "Where?"

"Up there." Morgan James pointed to where the

basket of the balloon had come down, stuck like an apple on the Devil's Backbone which rose sharply up from the beaver pond.

"Tell him to come down immediately," said Annabel Lee.

Peter Drummond dropped out a rope to a ledge on the Devil's Backbone below the basket. He dropped down on the rope like a sailor coming down the rigging. "Morgan James," he shouted. "Can you hear me?"

"I hear you," said Morgan James. "Tell everybody to come down. Annabel Lee wants to get married."

"The Preacher wants to go to Washington with the Frenchmen. He's never been there. He says it's his last chance. The wind is coming up and the basket is almost loose. With a little more gas they can take off."

"He can't go without marrying us," said Annabel Lee.

Peter Drummond shouted up to the balloon. The Preacher shouted back. "He says he'll marry you now if you're ready," said Peter Drummond.

"I'm ready," said Annabel Lee and took Morgan James firmly by the hand.

"He says 'Dearly Beloved, we are gathered here today,' " shouted Peter Drummond. "And he says if there be no man to step forward with reason that this should not go forward then we will go forward."

They looked around on the chance that somebody

might appear from the woods. Nobody showed up.

"He says that we may now proceed," shouted Peter Drummond.

"Good," said Annabel Lee and straightened her dress and flicked off the mud from her bosom.

"He wants to know who is giving this woman and I said I am," shouted Peter Drummond.

"And a perfect stranger," said Annabel Lee's mother.

"Be quiet, Momma. Just imagine you're in church."

" 'And do you, Annabel Lee,' he says," shouted Peter Drummond, " 'take this man Morgan James as your lawful wedded husband?' "

"I do," shouted Annabel Lee so that even the Preacher in the basket on top of the Devil's Backbone should have heard her.

"She does," shouted Peter Drummond to the Preacher. " 'And do you, Morgan James,' he says," shouted Peter Drummond, " 'take this woman Annabel Lee as your lawful wedded wife to have and to hold, et cetera?' "

"I do," said Morgan James.

"Louder," said Annabel Lee.

"I do," shouted Morgan James, cupping his hands to make sure the Preacher heard.

"He does," shouted Peter Drummond to the Preacher.

And then SUDDENLY the balloon gave a lurch and was off, moving up very fast. It happened just like that.

"Darn," said Annabel Lee. "He never had a chance to say IT. I just know I'll never get married now."

"I could spit sour," said Annabel Lee's mother.

"But it was good practice," said Morgan James trying to be helpful and comforting her as she sobbed on his shoulder.

5.

That next morning breakfast was as usual. Morgan James was pleased to note that Annabel Lee had not lost her touch, and her mother seemed especially anxious to please Peter Drummond. As she said, he was as close to a Lord as she had ever got, or was likely to get.

Peter Drummond was more than pleased and even expansive for him. "I am indebted," he said as he reached in his pocket. "I have been cherishing these for a long time, and I promised myself that I would not put them to ground until I found paradise."

"Now isn't that a pretty thing to say, Annabel Lee?" said her mother.

"They are ramp sets," said Peter Drummond. "So that no matter where I wander I shall know where to come to find kind hospitality — and ramps."

"Imagine that!" said Annabel Lee's mother. "After he wanders he's going to come back."

"Ramps!" said Annabel Lee in disgust, "and besides you don't plant ramps. They just grow."

"These will be planted," said Peter Drummond. "To-day."

"Where's the Almanac?" said Annabel Lee. "Let me look. They're like onions. And the moon's going down — and it doesn't come up until the fourteenth, that's the day after tomorrow."

"That's all right," said Peter Drummond. "We'll plant the ramps the day after tomorrow."

"Wait a minute," said Annabel Lee. "The day after tomorrow the moon is in Leo. You can't do it then."

"Come now," said Peter Drummond.

"You want to hear what it says, don't you? It says: 'Seed planted when the moon or earth is in Leo, which is a Barren Fiery Sign, will die, as it is only favorable to the destruction of noxious growth. Trim no trees or vines when the moon or earth is in Leo, for they will surely die.' "

"Sounds pretty bad to me," said Morgan James.

"Stay out of this, Morgan James," said Peter Drummond. "This is between me and Annabel Lee and the Almanac. What happens after Leo?"

"Let's see," said Annabel Lee. "It's Virgo. Now listen to this."

"I know it will be better, Mr. Drummond," said Annabel Lee's mother.

Annabel Lee continued: " 'Seed planted when the

91

earth is in Virgo, which is a Barren Sign, will not grow.' "

"Good Lord," said Peter Drummond, "be reasonable, Annabel Lee. How does anything grow?"

"Nature is Bountiful, Mr. Drummond," said Annabel Lee firmly. "Think of the queen bee, Mr. Drummond, and the males."

"They have nothing to do but lay down their lives for the queen," said Morgan James.

"Now how did you know that?" said Annabel Lee. "I would not have guessed you knew that."

"Just picked it up someplace, here or there."

"I think," said Annabel Lee's mother, "Mr. Drummond should just go ahead and plant those ramps wherever and whenever he wishes."

"Momma!" said Annabel Lee. "You wouldn't get up in the morning if you didn't know where the moon lay!"

"Mr. Drummond," said Annabel Lee's mother, "is a Lord and he lives by different moons than ordinary folk. But you know, Mr. Drummond, I was just looking at you sitting there opposite Morgan James and you and Morgan James are look-alikes. Come here, Annabel Lee, and look. Now you two just sit like that, nose to nose and chin to chin. And you both need haircuts dreadful."

So Morgan James and Peter Drummond sat there like that, nose to nose and chin to chin. Peter Drummond winked at Morgan James.

"Well, maybe," said Annabel Lee, squinting. "Morgan James has that same kind of Lord-like look and sometimes I think he thinks he's one for the way he acts."

"It's what Abelia said," said Peter Drummond. "She told me that Morgan James was like a Lord, didn't I think."

"Abelia said that?" said Morgan James, turning his nose and chin away.

"And who is Abelia?" said Annabel Lee.

"Just a girl," said Morgan James.

"And I suppose that's the way you talk about me, that I'm just a girl."

"I'm trying to think," said Morgan James thoughtfully, "how I would put it. I know I wouldn't say 'Just a girl.' Maybe I might say 'A girl I know' or maybe 'A girl I know very well' or maybe 'A girl who lives in the mountains and loves me.' "

"I don't imagine you would ever say, 'Annabel Lee is the woman I love.' You would never say that, would you, Morgan James?"

"I don't know anybody that well to say that to, except you, and there wouldn't be any point in saying it to you, now would there?"

"And while we're talking about you, Morgan James, what were you doing with that pedlar who tried to burn our house down?"

"Now, Annabel Lee," said her mother. "I am going to cut Mr. Drummond's hair and I don't want you to

93

make me nervous nor Morgan James either. Men come and men go, like tomcats, Annabel Lee, and you better get used to it."

"What were you doing with the pedlar, Morgan James?" said Annabel Lee.

"I was fleeing from the Amish. They wanted to bag me."

"Bag you?" said Peter Drummond. "That's a hunting expression."

"Keep your head still," said Annabel Lee's mother. "I think I found the ear."

"It's an Amish custom. They put a girl and a boy in a bag and shake 'em up, and if they come out still talking to each other, they get married. It's an old Amish custom," said Morgan James, looking for more biscuits.

"Is it?" said Annabel Lee. "There are no more biscuits and probably won't be. And who was this girl? Was this Abelia in the bag?"

"What are you talking about, Annabel Lee? I never got in the bag. It's why I left. I was only there because I didn't want to go to Scotland. But that was another girl. I mean in Scotland."

"I don't know about the other ear, Mr. Drummond, but this ear I found is a handsome one," said Annabel Lee's mother.

"This is truly an amazing tale," said Peter Drummond. "Keep on him, Annabel Lee."

"We'll come to the girl in Scotland, Morgan James," she said. "But first the girl in the bag."

"That's what I was trying to tell you, Annabel Lee. She never got in the bag. I never got in the bag. Nobody got in the bag. But if you want to know the name of the girl who wanted to get in the bag, her name was Inga."

"Ha!" said Annabel Lee. "Just a girl named Inga."

"She wasn't just a girl," said Morgan James.

"Ha!" said Annabel Lee. "She was not just a girl. She was something special."

"If I had gotten into that bag with Inga I would have been torn to bits. I would have been shredded," said Morgan James.

"Oh, I'm sorry, Mr. Drummond. Did that hurt? I cut off a piece of that handsome ear. I knew I would. I never heard such a story. He's always going backwards. Make him start at the beginning, Annabel Lee."

"We're doing fine, Momma. Morgan James is pouring out his life to me. It's just hard for him."

"Tell him to take the cork out of the bottle. It will pour better."

"Now why were you with the Amish, Morgan James?" asked Annabel Lee patiently.

"Because I had to flee Philadelphia, of course. Nobody is interested in this, Annabel Lee."

"I am almost all ears, Morgan James," said Peter Drummond. "Pray continue."

"That's very funny, Mr. Drummond," said Annabel Lee's mother. "Did you hear what Mr. Drummond said, Annabel Lee? 'Almost all ears.' I would have put that last piece back, Mr. Drummond, but it fell on the floor and I couldn't find it."

"Please do not concern yourself," said Peter Drummond. "Do not leave us in suspense, Morgan James."

"I was to take a ship from Philadelphia to Canada and from Canada to Scotland to claim my inheritance and marry a girl hand-picked."

"Well, I never," said Annabel Lee's mother. "If pigs could fly!"

"Just a girl from Scotland, I suppose. What was her name?"

"It's what I can't remember, but it was a very funny name."

"And this inheritance in Scotland, Morgan James. It was not attractive?" asked Peter Drummond.

"Look at it this way," said Morgan James. "I was going to have to live there. I was going to be a Lord. Among a whole lot of other Lords who would look at me as some stranger just because whoever should have been the Lord had died before his time. And marry a girl hand-picked."

"Right," said Peter Drummond. "But what did your family say?"

"My father wanted nothing to do with it. This was my mother's family anyway. And she wanted me to go back and that was how the ship from Philadelphia was arranged."

"I see it," said Peter Drummond. "Scotland is still Scotland. All the male heirs had tapped out and then the inheritance came to your mother, who could not take claim because she was female and it passed to you."

"I can understand," said Annabel Lee, "why you wouldn't want to go to a country like that where they treat women like that. Imagine!"

"And what is your mother's maiden name?" asked Peter Drummond.

"I can't remember that either," said Morgan James. "You see it was all in this letter from the lawyer, or whatever he called himself, and the family tree, in Scotland."

"Solicitor," said Peter Drummond.

"That's it. Solicitor. Anyway, it's all in the letter with all the names of the family way back. I do remember one — Doric the Dane."

"A famous name in Scotland," said Peter Drummond. "If you would believe all you were told, everybody in Scotland is descended from the great Doric the Dane. Indeed my grandfather used to talk of him."

"I'm going to get a mirror, Mr. Drummond, so you can see, and then I think you should shave."

Peter Drummond looked in the mirror. "I must say it is a transformation. And I might shave — to be presentable in the presence of our real Lord Morgan James."

"I used to shave my late husband, Mr. Drummond," said Annabel Lee's mother.

"It is a kind offer, but I will decline," said Peter Drummond as he looked at his ears in the mirror. "But," he turned suddenly to Morgan James, "where is this letter with all the names? I want to see it. You have aroused all my memories of my great country."

"But that's just it. I've lost it," said Morgan James, "and I don't know where. It was in a waterproof pouch and I always had it. I remember I even had it when I was with the pedlar. And then I just haven't seen it."

"I never saw it, silly," said Annabel Lee.

"Silly! That's it. The name of the girl in Scotland was Killie, except no Y. It was I-E. Sarah Killie was her name."

Peter Drummond jumped up. "But that's too much, Morgan James. Sarah Killie. I, too, was to marry a Killie girl. It was to bring our two families together. Now you must find that letter, Morgan James. What did you do when you left the pedlar?"

"He was running away from the Indians," said Annabel Lee. "Those poor miserable Indians."

"Then it could be anywheres," said Peter Drummond.

"It couldn't fall off," said Morgan James. "It was on a belt I wore about my waist on the skin."

"Think, Morgan James," said Annabel Lee.

"Think, Morgan James," said Peter Drummond.

"When he arrived here he wasn't wearing anything except those bites," said Annabel Lee's mother.

"The beaver house!" said Annabel Lee. "The letter is in the beaver house, Momma!"

"No," said Morgan James.

"We go to the beaver house," said Peter Drummond.

"No," said Morgan James.

"I want to know about this Sarah Killie," said Annabel Lee.

"To the beaver house," said Peter Drummond.

And so they went.

Morgan James did not want to do it. It had been different with the Indians after him. But now it was Annabel Lee because she wanted to know more about Sarah Killie. It was Annabel Lee's mother who wanted to know more about Doric. It was Peter Drummond who just wanted to know more.

And so Morgan James took a deep breath and dove in. He found the entrance and got his head above water. There didn't seem to be anyone there. He couldn't hear any breathing or scratching either. He crawled onto the first level and then slowly onto the second level. He reached to find his clothes and then the pants, and then the belt with the pouch. It was there. And as quickly as he could with the belt in his hand he slid out backwards into the water.

When he got back to the shore Peter Drummond took the belt and went to a dry spot with Annabel Lee and her mother. Nobody even said "Thank you."

Peter Drummond took the letter. He looked at the signature first. "Yes, I knew it. Old Fergusson."

"If pigs could fly," said Annabel Lee's mother. "You know the man."

Peter Drummond did not answer as he read the letter and talked to himself. "Yes," he said. "Um," he said. "So that's it," he said. "Of course," he said. "I knew it. That name Killie."

"Will you read the letter, Mr. Drummond?" said Annabel Lee. "Nothing can be told from that. Is Morgan James a Lord and does he have to marry this Sarah Killie?"

"He is not and he does not have to."

"It was just made up," said Annabel Lee.

"No, it was not, Annabel Lee. You see, I am the new Lord MacLaren. But if we hadn't met as we have and I had not known of this, then Morgan James would have been the new Lord MacLaren. But he will be, of course, when I die, if I die without issue, as I shall, for I am much too old to marry now."

Peter Drummond spread out a piece of paper with a chart. "Now this," he said, "is the best way to understand it."

James Dobie, Sr.   (Lord MacLaren)

James Dobie, Jr.   Peter Dobie   Margaret Dobie

Morgan James

"Where are you, Mr. Drummond? I don't see you," said Annabel Lee's mother.

"There, where it says 'Peter Dobie.' That's my name, my real name. But I had pecuniary difficulties and it seemed convenient to put a notice in the Harrisburg paper of my demise, and I took the name of Peter Drummond."

"It doesn't make a word of sense to me," said Annabel Lee's mother. "I'm glad, Annabel Lee, that you weren't married by that preacher. It probably would not have taken."

Morgan James studied the chart. "Then you're Peter Dobie and my mother's brother."

"And your uncle, Morgan James," said Annabel Lee.

"I told you they were look-alikes," said Annabel Lee's mother.

"Now here, you see at the top of the chart 'James Dobie, Sr., Lord MacLaren' — my father. And he had three children — James, Peter, and Margaret. And when my father died, my brother James became Lord MacLaren. Now, when he died six months ago the title would have come to me, but they thought I was dead so it went to Margaret and through her to Morgan James."

"And will you wear kilts?" asked Annabel Lee.

"There will be times," said Peter Drummond, Peter Dobie, Lord MacLaren.

"Morgan James has very good limbs," said Annabel Lee.

"I'm sure he has," said Peter Dobie, Lord MacLaren.

"I am not wearing any kilts," said Morgan James. "My mother suggested it and it's one reason I'm here."

"For me," said Annabel Lee, "just for me."

"Maybe, just for you, but it won't be for long, you understand, Annabel Lee."

"Now you people will have to come visit me," said Lord MacLaren, "and in the meantime, Morgan James, you can manage our property in the Ohio Territories. That's what I came over to do, but I found them full of Indians and with the War it was not a Salutary Place to be. Then my brother James and I fell out so — one thing led to another and that was how I came to be with the Preacher."

"But if it hadn't been for my wanting to be married, then Morgan James would not have found the Preacher and then you wouldn't have found out you were a Lord," said Annabel Lee.

"And those Indians who were chasing me are part of the story, too, because that's how I got to the beaver pond in the first place," said Morgan James. "Nobody ever remembers how I was chased by whooping Indians."

"I know that," said Annabel Lee, "and I've been wanting to talk to you about it." She said it sort of meanly too.

"You mean how dangerous it was for me to be chased by them and how bravely I faced it?"

"I do not," said Annabel Lee, "and I do not know

102

how you could bring it up in public." And she just walked ahead alone. Morgan James looked at Annabel Lee's mother. He looked at Lord MacLaren. Both of them just looked away as if they did not want anything to do with him. For Morgan James it spoiled the whole day and lots of days before and all the days that were to come if they ever did. It was a dark mystery. And especially dark because nothing new had happened or had been said. The Indians had chased him into the beaver pond. And no matter how many times he went over it he always ended up in the beaver pond with the Indians whooping all around.

Morgan James could feel the gathering storm all afternoon, both in Annabel Lee and in the sky and in the air. There was no breeze and the air became heavier. It was unnatural — more like summer than the end of November. Annabel Lee's mother was in the kitchen. Lord MacLaren had shaved and with his haircut he really looked the Lord. He kept rereading the letter.

Morgan James and Annabel Lee were on the swing on the porch. They were not talking.

It had become suddenly almost dark with black clouds building castles in the sky.

"See the castles in the sky," said Morgan James, "with the walls and towers and maybe even flags flying where that white is."

"It is what I always wanted, to be in a castle like

that," said Annabel Lee, in a soft slow mournful voice. "But I must face it."

Morgan James hesitated. He could ask her what it was that she must face, and he was curious to know, but on the other hand he decided to not pursue it.

"I must be brave," said Annabel Lee, sitting up straight on the swing and looking courageously ahead.

"Certainly," said Morgan James. He felt on pretty safe ground there. You should always be brave.

"And that's all you have to say, just I must be brave. That's all?" Annabel Lee gave a push to the swing so her nut-brown legs could stretch out in front of her.

"Well," said Morgan James. He wanted to leave the door open in case there was something more that he wanted to say. He would have liked to say how much he admired her nut-brown legs, but that might be inflammatory. And besides he didn't know what they were talking about.

"I don't know how you could have brought up those Indians the way you did."

Morgan James felt new life and fresh air. He was on firm ground now. "You mean the Indians who chased me whooping into the beaver pond?"

There was a burst of thunder in the distance and the whole castle suddenly filled with lightning.

"I do," said Annabel Lee. "If it hadn't been for those Indians we would never have met."

"Right!" said Morgan James. "That's what I've been saying."

"So you admit it," said Annabel Lee. "You don't love me."

It was like the thunderbolt in the castle. "I don't?" said Morgan James.

"You were just afraid of those miserable Indians. You weren't looking for me."

Morgan James shook his head. "I didn't know you were there."

"That's just what I've been saying, Morgan James. In your whole life you never looked for Me. You didn't get on your white charger and say 'I'm going to find Annabel Lee' did you?"

These were deep, deep waters. Morgan James decided to go back to what was known. "The Indians were chasing me," he said.

"They chase lots of people," said Annabel Lee. "And now you are going to leave me."

"I am?"

"Well, aren't you?" said Annabel Lee. "Now you don't have to go to Scotland. You can just go home."

"No," said Morgan James. "There are two reasons. One is that my father is a printer in Camden, New Jersey, and he wants me to be a printer in Camden, New Jersey, and wear a printer's apron."

"And what's wrong with that?"

"It's too niggly-piggly. Those tiny tiny pieces of type and inky, too. Have you ever seen a typographical error?"

"So you were going to wear an apron in Camden or

a kilt in Scotland? Poor Morgan James. You can put your arm around me and you'd be more comfortable."

Morgan James did so. It was much more comfortable.

KA-BOOM! The house shook. And then out on the main road in the sudden flash of light they saw a white horse — a big white horse — rear up and they thought they saw a figure go flying off.

"See!" said Annabel Lee. The white horse was running in terror toward them. The loose reins were flapping in front of him.

"Oh, the poor thing," said Annabel Lee. "I'll get him. Horses love me." She ran down from the porch to where the horse was now quietly munching at the grass. She caught the bridle where it trailed along the ground. "Lovely fellow, lovely fellow," she said as she kissed his soft nose and stroked his white neck.

"Did you ever see such a saddle?" said Morgan James. "And look! It says U.S. Army. And it has this saddlebag with a lock on it."

Lord MacLaren appeared and they told him what they knew. "We must get a wagon," he said. "The rider must have been thrown and is out upon the road someplace."

They put the white horse in the barn and the three of them took the wagon out to the main road. The storm was over. The trees dripped coolly. The air was sweet.

Annabel Lee pushed close to Morgan James. "And you're never going to leave," she said.

Lord MacLaren smiled out of his new Lord-like shaven face. "The storm must be o'er."

"What storm?" said Annabel Lee.

"I just wonder where that rider is," said Morgan James. "He must be an officer with important dispatches."

They didn't find him at first, but then they saw him stretched out along the side of the road. He was unconscious. Lord MacLaren took his pulse. "He's alive, but we'll have to be careful. You don't know what's broken." They moved him as gently as they could onto the wagon. Annabel Lee found his cap with gold braid and dusted it off.

He was still unconscious when they put him on the bed in the kitchen.

"Such a handsome young man," said Annabel Lee's mother. "And look at those locks. Locks of raven hair is what they be, Annabel Lee."

"I know," said Annabel Lee as she stroked the handsome young man's head.

Morgan James had the terrible, terrible, selfish thought that he hoped the handsome young man was at least mortally injured.

"And did you ever see such a uniform, Momma? All that gold on the blue jacket. And those tight white pants and the black boots to the knee."

"They'll have to be cut off," said Annabel Lee's mother.

"Oh, you couldn't, Momma!"

"I'll cut 'em off," said Morgan James.

"Let's hope it's not necessary," said Lord Mac-Laren. "Maybe this will help." He had one of his ramps. He rubbed it under the young man's nose.

"Maybe I should bite his hand," said Morgan James, "and say 'Rise Whoever You Are.'"

"No, look," said Lord MacLaren, "he stirs."

"He is trying to speak," said Annabel Lee's mother.

The young man's eyes opened. "Major William Remington, Second Dragoons, U.S. Army."

"We won't have to cut off his beautiful tight white pants now," said Annabel Lee.

"My saddlebag," said Major William Remington, Second Dragoons, U.S. Army. "Bring me my saddle-bag."

When Morgan James came back with the saddlebag the Major was sitting up, but he looked very poorly, even if it wasn't poorly enough, Morgan James thought. His head was bandaged, and even though it covered his raven locks the bandage was more dashing than necessary. Morgan James was sure that Annabel Lee had put it on. And they had taken his jacket off and draped it around his shoulders in a ridiculous way. And there was no doubt that Annabel Lee had done that, too.

"Now take this," said Annabel Lee's mother to the

patient. It was Dr. Coffin's Restorative Elixir.

"Where did you get that, Momma?"

"It's good to always have a little bit around."

Lord MacLaren smelled the bottle. "If I'm any judge it's ninety proof — and I am. It will kill him or cure him."

The Major took a big gulp. "Oh, my word, sir, that's powerful stuff." He started to cough and then made a face in agony and sank back.

"I'm afraid you have broken your shoulder and you must have a concussion too," said Lord MacLaren.

"My saddlebag," said the Major bravely. "Give me my saddlebag." With a key from around his neck he opened it. "Now," he said, and he read from a parchment he held in front of him. "To whom it may Concern. The Bearer of this is Major William Remington, Second Dragoons, U.S. Army. He carries Extraordinary Documents to General Andrew Jackson before New Orleans. He must be shown every Courtesy, Assistance, Cooperation in the Execution of his Duties. Signed the White House, James Madison, President of the United States of America."

"If pigs could fly!" said Annabel Lee's mother.

"These dispatches must reach General Jackson immediately. The fate of the Nation may rest on them," said the Major.

"One thing for certain, Major, is that you can't do it," said Lord MacLaren.

"And who, sir, are you?"

109

"Lord MacLaren, at your service."

"He's a British Spy. Shoot him," said the Major, looking around the room for the people he usually had with him to shoot spies.

"Not in the house," said Annabel Lee's mother.

The Major looked at Morgan James. "And you, who are you?"

"Morgan James, sir."

"A good and loyal American?"

"I am, sir."

"Then you must do it. You must go in my place. But you can't go like that. You will put on my uniform and I will write a letter for you to carry so that the Citizens of this Country will know to show you every Courtesy, Assistance, Cooperation in the Execution of your Duties. The Ladies will leave the room."

"But you can't go, Morgan James. You said you would never leave," said Annabel Lee.

"Please, Ladies," said the Major and motioned them from the room. They went.

With as much care as possible Lord MacLaren and Morgan James took off the Major's uniform. Morgan James was pleased to notice that he didn't look like much without it. In fact he had a big hole in one sock. Morgan James felt better about leaving the Major there under those circumstances. And if Annabel Lee's mother gave him a haircut there wouldn't be any problems at all.

"If pigs could fly," said Lord MacLaren, as he

helped Morgan James into his blue jacket with the gold braid. "You should see yourself now." The pants were dangerously tight. It must be, Morgan James thought, that soldiers wore them that way to cut down on the bleeding if they got shot.

"The cap, sir," said Lord MacLaren.

"Bring in the Ladies if you please," said the Major. "We will need witnesses for the Swearing In. American Citizens," scowling at Lord MacLaren.

"Oh!" cried Annabel Lee when she saw him, "Oh!" She covered her face with her apron. Then she peeked. "Oh!" she cried.

"If pigs could . . ." said Annabel Lee's mother.

"I've already covered that," said Lord MacLaren.

"You will raise your Right Hand, Morgan James, and Repeat after me, 'I, Morgan James, swear to Uphold the Laws and Defend the Honor of the United States of America!' " said the Major.

"I do," said Morgan James.

"You're not getting married, sir."

"Can you marry people, Major?" said Annabel Lee.

"No, ma'am, I cannot."

"I was just wondering," said Annabel Lee, beginning to cry again.

"Where was I?" said the Major.

Morgan James still had his right hand up. "I, Morgan James," he said.

"That's enough," said the Major. "The important thing is I am making you a Volunteer Captain, Second

111

Dragoons, U.S. Army. And here is the saddlebag. And here is the key to wear around your neck. To horse!" said the Major.

"No!" cried Annabel Lee.

Morgan James tried to hug her and at the same time he didn't want her tears to tarnish the gold braid on his jacket.

"You can't," cried Annabel Lee.

"I must," said Morgan James. He wanted to tell Annabel Lee's mother to be sure to cut the Major's Raven Locks.

"Robert Fulton should have one of the new steamboats waiting for you in Memphis to take you to New Orleans," said the Major. "God Speed."

"I'll take care of things around here," said Lord MacLaren.

"To horse!" said the Major, "to horse!"

6.

Morgan James stopped when he reached the main road. They were still standing in front of the house. He knew they would want to see him go off in style. "Prance," he said. The horse did a little prance, but not much. He was sure the Major would have a horse that could prance. "Prance," he said. The horse did a little prance again. Maybe the horse had to have a name, and if he knew Major William Remington, Second Dragoons, U.S. Army, it would be a fancy name. "Prance, Ulysses!" he said. And Ulysses pranced, and darn near pranced Morgan James on his tail. He was glad that they were far enough away to see just the big part of the prance and not the little part where he had to throw his arms around Ulysses' neck.

It was a grand ride in the falling night. He would like to see some Indians come along now. His saddle-bag was full of gold coins. On one side of the saddle was a long sword and on the other a rifle in a leather case. Morgan James walked Ulysses a bit. He trotted Ulysses a bit. And he galloped Ulysses a bit. In no time he was on the top of the mountain above Studgeville where the Senator had practiced his speechmaking.

It seemed a prudent place to stop. Morgan James took out the sword and cried "Hurrah!" and cut down weeds. He took a scrap of paper from the saddlebag and stuck it to a tree for target practice. As he turned there was a *Ka-Boom* and there was a hole in the scrap of paper.

He didn't even have to look. "Abelia," he said, "where are you? I know it's you."

"Over here," she said, as she came out from behind a tree. "You scared me, whipping that sword around like that. You could have hurt somebody."

"What are you doing here? I thought you went to New Orleans with the Volunteers."

"I was on my way," said Abelia, "but one day we were on a line of march along the river and I had to pee something awful and they found out I was a girl and sent me home."

"I'm sorry," said Morgan James. "But you will come with me. I go to New Orleans with important Dispatches from President Madison to General Andrew Jackson before New Orleans."

"You really want me to come?" said Abelia. "I don't think anybody wants me."

"I should have a scout in my position," said Morgan

114

James. "I am ordering you as a Citizen of the United States to Assist me in every way and to Show me all Courtesy."

"I don't have a horse," said Abelia.

"That will be taken care of," said Morgan James. "We can ride double to Studgeville and there we will find a mount for you. To horse!"

It was well that Annabel Lee did not see Abelia riding behind Morgan James down the mountain. She had her arms tightly around his waist and a tear or two were making tracks on her dirty cheeks.

And who should the first person they met be but Senator Bagful riding a handsome black stallion. The Senator hailed them. "Ah, Captain, glad to see you. I heard that a detachment would be coming from Washington."

"I come from Washington but on a Special Mission from the President."

"It's Morgan James, isn't it?" said the Senator, looking at him closely.

"Captain Morgan James, Second Dragoons, United States Army." He showed his papers. "And I require a horse for my Scout."

"I am certain that we can find a suitable mount in Studgeville. You understand that our recent — uh — recent misunderstanding in Seldom Seen was just politics. Just politics, sir, and nothing personal."

"Of course," said Morgan James. "I want your horse — and saddle."

"But — bu-bu-but . . ." said the Senator.

"You saw the Commission, Senator," said Morgan James. "I am to be shown every Courtesy, Assistance, Cooperation in the Execution of my Duties."

"But Captain, Saturn and I have been together through Thick and Thin. And Compensation, Captain?"

Morgan James could have parted with some of his gold coins but he didn't think the Senator would properly appreciate them. Instead he wrote out an I.O.U. for "One horse received (Saturn)" signed "President James Madison, per Captain Morgan James."

"You will tell the President of this when you see him, won't you?" said the Senator, standing plaintively in the dusty street stroking Saturn sadly.

"I may," said Morgan James. "To horse!"

"That was really slick," said Abelia as they rode out of town. "I think Saturn's a pretty name, don't you?"

"It's all right," said Morgan James.

They camped that night in a pine grove some way off from the road.

"Did that preacher ever get you married?" asked Abelia.

"He tried mighty hard, but the wind was against him," said Morgan James.

"You couldn't hear him, I guess," said Abelia, as she munched on some dried beef. "I hope that doesn't happen to me, not the wind, I mean, blowing away the vows, but the getting married. I don't like men — ex-

116

cept you and Peter Drummond. And I don't like all women or girls."

"But you're going to become a woman, Abelia, a grand woman."

"They're the worst. And maybe I will and maybe I won't. I don't have any titties at all. You know, I think we're being followed, Morgan James. I've had that feeling all day, and even more now since it got dark."

"And why would anyone want to follow us?"

"All your talk of Dispatches to General Jackson and taking that Senator's horse."

"That was just the proper Courtesy and Assistance that the President wants. He said so in his Commission."

"I'm going to snoop anyway," said Abelia, picking up her rifle. "You stay here. You need to be protected."

"Promise me," said Morgan James, "you won't shoot anybody."

"Not unless it's absolutely necessary," said Abelia and disappeared into the night.

Morgan James was almost dozing when Abelia returned. "I saw them," she said. "I could have done them all in."

Morgan James was awake now. "Who?"

"All of them," she said. "There was the Senator. And that tubby man."

"Hamilton Roller."

"That one, and another one. A scraggly man. And I

heard every word they said. They have a scheme. They want those Dispatches and the Senator wants his horse."

"Never," said Morgan James. "Over my dead body."

"It is to be over *my* dead body. I should have shot them all. It has to do with the cotton market. They think the Dispatches will make the cotton market go up or go down and if they find out before anyone else they will make a bundle one way or t'other. That's what the tubby man said."

"But what's the scheme?" asked Morgan James, pulling on his shiny black boots.

"The Senator said I was mean and dangerous," said Abelia, "and the scraggly man was to get me. Do you think I'm mean and dangerous?"

"And how would they get the Dispatches?"

"They don't want to kill you. You're a U.S. Army Officer. But with you alone they think they can steal the Dispatches."

"It's deep waters," said Morgan James.

"I'm hungry," said Abelia.

The Scraggly Man stayed close to them all day. Once he even came up beside them. "Howdy," he said. He had a scraggly beard and scraggly hair and his clothes were scraggly too.

"Howdy," Morgan James said.

The Scraggly Man looked closely at Abelia. "Howdy," he said.

Abelia didn't say anything. She just looked as mean and dangerous as she could.

"Your young friend isn't very sociable, Captain."

"He's pretty quiet. He likes to size people up."

"Meaning what, Captain?" said the Scraggly Man.

"Meaning I like to size people up before I socialize," said Abelia.

"I guess I get the lay of things around here," said the Scraggly Man. "There's a town up here a piece where I've got to see some people. Maybe you know it — Falling Springs?"

"That's where we're going, too," said Morgan James. "It's where this young man comes from. I'm just riding home with him."

Abelia looked at Morgan James and frowned.

"Is that so?" said the Scraggly Man. "Well, maybe I'll see you there. And take care of that horse, Captain, he's a good 'un."

"I'll do that," said Morgan James.

Abelia stuck out her tongue at the back of the Scraggly Man as he rode away. "And you're going to leave me in Falling Springs?"

"It's deep waters, Abelia, very deep," said Morgan James.

"But who's going to take care of you if you're all alone? You saw that man looking at your saddlebags."

"You're going to have to become a girl, Abelia."

Abelia pulled her horse up short. "But you can't do that to me, Morgan James. You wouldn't do that."

119

"The President of the United States says that all Citizens should give all Assistance and Cooperation and Courtesy to me in the Execution of my Duties."

Abelia half began to cry. "I can't," she wailed, "I simply can't."

Morgan James was pleased that her tears only hardened and strengthened him in his resolve.

Falling Springs was bustling that day. Morgan James rode tall through the people and horses and wagons ignoring the snivels of Abelia. The Valley Inn and Tavern looked half respectable — the Inn part being respectable and the Tavern being not. The lady who ran the Inn was just what Morgan James had hoped for. Her name was Mrs. MacPherson. She was short and round but firm with no nonsense about her apple red cheeks.

"And what can I do for you, Captain?" she said, looking out of the corner of her eyes at Abelia, who had stopped sniveling and was only damp and sullen.

"I'll tell you my problem, ma'am. My sister here ran away from home and I'm bringing her back, but I can't take her back like this." Both Morgan James and Mrs. MacPherson looked at poor Abelia, who looked like something that no self-respecting cat would have brought in.

"I can understand that well enough, Captain. She needs fixing from stem to stern."

"I hate you," said Abelia to Morgan James.

"Don't you worry, Captain. I can handle her. I had

one once like that. I've still got her clothes upstairs and they'll fit this one fine, but I've got to have something for them, you understand."

Morgan James took two gold coins from the saddle-bag.

Mrs. MacPherson allowed her eyes to light up. "It will be a pleasure, Captain."

"From stem to stern," said Morgan James.

Mrs. MacPherson took Abelia firmly by an ear and marched her upstairs.

"I'll get you for this," said Abelia through clenched teeth to Morgan James. And she was not fooling either.

"Just remember," said Morgan James, catching her eye, "when you come down I want you to be the sweet lovable Abelia that I've always known. All girl."

Abelia seemed to catch the message before she was yanked by an ear upstairs.

While Abelia was being done Morgan James bought a handsome two-wheeler with a roof for Abelia to drive. The Senator's horse looked very ashamed in the traces but Morgan James figured he would get used to it. Morgan James was rocking on the porch when Abelia came down.

He didn't see her come out but he heard this strange honeyed voice behind him. "Why, brother dear, I hope I didn't keep you rocking while I did myself." It was well that Morgan James was sitting down. It was not just a transformation. She was almost blond with her hair washed and ribbons and the beginning of a graceful neck coming out of the top of her flowery dress, and pantaloons, too, peeking out from the bottom of her dress.

Mrs. MacPherson still had sleeves rolled up from her scrubbing. "I don't know when she ran away but I can guarantee that not a drop of soap and water has touched her in that time, Captain. I had to go down almost to the bone, I did."

"And now aren't I, dear brother, the sweet Abelia you remember?"

"You is, I mean you are," said Morgan James, who could do without the 'dear brother' bit. "Well, I thank you, Mrs. MacPherson. We are indebted to you."

"The pantaloons may come off. I tied them up the best I could. My girl had more on her bones than this one. You'll just have to pull 'em up and tie 'em up again."

"I'll do that," said Morgan James.

"My dear brother is so dear," said Abelia.

"I hope you can drive this thing, Abelia," said Morgan James as he handed her into the two-wheeler. "And you can cut out the 'dear brother.'"   -

"I just don't know if I can. That big big horse and just little old me. *Hi-yup!*" She gave the Senator's horse a whack on the rear with the leather and she was off like a rocket down the Main Street of Falling Springs, scattering chickens and pigs and people and wagons. Morgan James stood open-mouthed in the dust wondering what he had let loose upon the world.

122

"Well, I declare," she said when he caught up with her out of town, "I was so frightened when we went through town like that. My heart was just going patty-patty-patty. It really was."

"I bet," said Morgan James.

"But you do think I look all right?" she said in her old voice. "I never looked like this before. I used to be on the inside looking out and now I'm on the outside looking at me, if you know what I mean."

The road seemed to get worse and worse as they went on until finally there was no road at all, or at least no bridge at all across a deep gorge.

"There must have been a washout," said Morgan James. "I'm going to ride up and take a look. That means reconnoiter."

"You better be careful," said Abelia. "I have a feeling that Scraggly Man is not far away."

Abelia sat properly in the two-wheeler feeling quite grand. She felt more comfortable alone dressed up like this. She stretched out her legs and admired her pantaloons peeking out from under her skirt.

And then it happened.

The Scraggly Man came slouching out of the woods toward her. "The little lady looks like she needs company," he said.

Abelia grabbed the rifle behind her. "Stay where you are. I'm no little lady."

"That's a dangerous weapon for a little lady," said the Scraggly Man and came closer.

"That's it," said Abelia in her most mean and dangerous snarl.

The Scraggly Man looked at her more closely and stopped. "I might have known the way you drove out of town that it was just a get-up."

"You have it," said Abelia and jumped down from the two-wheeler, keeping the gun on him all the time. But as she jumped her pantaloons fell down and tripped her up.

The Scraggly Man was on her in an instant. He kept his hands on her mouth so she couldn't cry out. In a moment he had her tied to a wheel. And then he wrapped the pantaloons about her head to keep her quiet.

"Gr-r-r-r," said Abelia.

Morgan James came back shortly.

"What do you think you're doing?" he said when he saw Abelia.

"Gr-r-r-r," she said.

The Scraggly Man stepped out from behind the two-wheeler where he had been hiding. He had his gun leveled at Morgan James. "Now, Captain, I want you to get down from that horse. And then I'm going to leave you right here. I'm going across the top of the old dam and you can sit here with the little lady which she ain't and wait for them to build you a new bridge."

"Gr-r-r-r," said Abelia.

Morgan James did get down and went over and

stood next to Abelia tied to the wheel. "You all right?" he said.

"Gr-r-r-r," she said.

The Scraggly Man set himself in the saddle. He patted the horse's neck. "He is a handsome one all right, Captain." He tipped his hat. "I'll be seeing you and the little lady," and he laughed.

"Gr-r-r-r," said Abelia.

They watched him stepping his horse carefully across the top of the dam. He had to be cautious because it was so narrow and on one side there was a very steep drop to the rocks of the river below.

Suddenly Morgan James ran forward. "Prance, Ulysses, prance!" And Ulysses did prance. The Scraggly Man was pitched head over heels over the edge onto the rocks below. Ulysses stood alone on the dam shaking his head proudly.

"I want to see him. I hope he's squished," said Abelia as Morgan James untied her from the wheel. "And look what he did to my pantaloons."

"Are you all right?"

"I'm all right. It wouldn't have happened if my pantaloons hadn't of fallen down."

They walked on top of the dam. The Scraggly Man lay broken on the rocks way below.

"He's squished all right," said Abelia. "You know, I've been thinking," she said as they walked back to the two-wheeler.

"About?"

"About going back to Falling Springs."

"I thought you were coming with me to New Orleans like you always wanted to," said Morgan James.

"They'll just send me back again like they did before. And I messed up trying to protect you. And if I go on like this I'll just end up squished like the Scraggly Man. That's what Mrs. MacPherson said and she's right."

"What's Mrs. MacPherson know about the Scraggly Man?" said Morgan James.

"Here, now tie them tight," said Abelia as she pulled on her pantaloons. "And he tore them, too. I told her my whole Life."

"You didn't."

"I did. You don't think she believed your cat-and-the-fiddle story about your sister?"

Morgan James was amazed that Mrs. MacPherson was so two-faced. "You made me out to be a liar, Abelia."

"You don't know how to lie a-tall. All you do is open your eyes wide like a rabbit. Mrs. MacPherson wants me to come live with her and help with the Inn. She thinks I'm smart and have self-reliance and am going to be beautiful."

"That's for sure," said Morgan James, "but I can't go all the way back to Falling Springs. I must push on."

"Just let me borrow the two-wheeler and I'll go back. You go on."

"I guess it's for the best," said Morgan James, "but I thought you didn't like Mrs. MacPherson."

"She's a no-nonsense woman, and that's how I'd be with young-uns, too."

She turned the two-wheeler around. She looked down at Morgan James. "Now you take care of yourself, Captain." Then she jumped down, stood on her tiptoes, and gave him a peck on the cheek. And then she was off very sedately, sitting very proper, and only lightly flicking the rear end of the Senator's horse now and then.

As Morgan James rode out across the dam he looked down toward the Scraggly Man, but he wasn't squished at all. He was standing up, shaking his fist. Morgan James was thankful that Abelia did not see it. She would have been most disappointed.

It wasn't far to Memphis, which was a pretty good-sized town. And a River. The biggest River he had ever seen, muddy and rolling as it went on its own way to the Ocean. But Mr. Fulton's boat was not there. It had blown up in Cincinnati, and New Orleans was almost a thousand miles away.

"You can take a keelboat, Captain," said the naval officer who had been there waiting for Mr. Fulton's new steamship.

"And how long would that be?" said Morgan James.

"Six or eight weeks. What with getting stuck on sandbars and you can't travel at night."

"My Dispatches must go forward faster than that."

"You could ride it, but it'll be a long one what with needing fresh horses, and you have to sleep. Even the Post Stage takes three weeks what with stopping for passengers and all."

"There will be no passengers," said Morgan James, and they went to the Postmaster.

"Impossible," said the Postmaster, who if he didn't know anything else knew the regulations. "The mail leaves at noon on Tuesdays and all the way along the line there are appointed times for pickup." He was a big bald man with a big stomach and two large gold watch chains that stretched across it. He looked at his watches continually as if he was anxious what the Time was doing behind his back. "This watch," he said, "is Memphis Time. And this watch is New Orleans Time. So I know what Time it is all the Time."

"There will be no mail. There will be no passengers," said Morgan James.

"But it's the Mail Coach," said the Postmaster. "If there's no mail, it's not the Mail Coach." He looked at his watch. "Right now it's one o'clock in New Orleans."

Morgan James showed him the Commission which he read very carefully and very slowly and over again, too. "These must be very important Dispatches, Captain."

"The Fate of the Nation, Mr. Postmaster," said Morgan James.

"But if the Mail Coach leaves now it won't be here

to leave on Tuesday and the Northbound one won't be back for ten days." He looked at his Memphis watch as if to make sure the world had not turned upside down.

"The Fate of the Nation," said Morgan James, "and take care of my horse. It is Government Property."

In this part of the country they still talk of the famous Post Stage that ran that January in 1815 from Memphis to New Orleans without stopping day or night. Of course it did stop to change horses, but that was all and it is not remembered. It is said that sometimes on a dark rainy night in the winter the Stage comes flying down the road with horses flecked white and the drivers flicking their whips in the air. It is even said that you can see the Captain of Dragoons upright inside the Stage. And it is always said that it was those Dispatches from the President to the General that won the War and kept this country Free.

It was after Midnight January 8, 1815, when Captain Morgan James arrived in New Orleans with his Fateful Dispatches. He staggered unsteadily from so long in the Mail Coach that had become home, but he did not let grass grow under his feet. He commandeered a horse and followed the crowd out to Cypress Swamps, where the battle was to be fought. It was not hard to find the General who was in charge of everything — moving guns here, setting up cotton bales there, moving troops everywhere. There were slouching deer-skinned volunteers from Tennessee. There were fancy Zouaves of the New Orleans Militia. There were the pirates of Jean Lafitte.

The General was tall with bushy jet-black hair and commanding eyes. Morgan James saluted: "A Dispatch from the President of the United States, sir."

"And how far away are the troops you brought, Captain?"

"There are no troops, sir," said Morgan James.

The General took the packet, put on his glasses, and read it carefully. Morgan James studied his face for the slightest clue or reaction of the great General. But the General was cool as a cucumber and revealed nothing. He stuck the Dispatch in the top of his boot.

"It was good of you to come, Morgan James," General Jackson said. "We need men like you, sir."

The Battle of New Orleans could now begin. The light was coming across the Cypress Swamp and gradually to the right was revealed a great wide plain.

"They will come from there," said the General, "and we will stop them here." He stood on a cotton bale and surveyed the scene. "I want you to station yourself here and let me know the first sign of their appearance." He gave Morgan James his own telescope and jumped down to oversee other parts of the defense. As he jumped down the Dispatch fell out of his boot. Morgan James went to pick it up for him, but the General had already stridden off. Morgan James knew he shouldn't do it, that it was not for him to see, but

130

he had risked Life and Limb and there was no way he was not going to peek:

> Dear General Jackson,
>   I write to you in great Haste as the Courier waits without. The Troops that you so urgently Requested and that I did Promise would be forthcoming cannot be Spared from the Niagara Frontier. I realize how dreadful the Odds are now against you, but I have Faith in your Abilities and that the Lord will not desert us in our hour of Need.
>   I am Respectfully, Sir, and with Great Esteem,
>   James Madison
>   PRESIDENT — UNITED STATES OF AMERICA

Then — all of a sudden — there was a cry of "Morgan James" and he saw a wagon approaching. Annabel Lee was driving in her bee bonnet! The Preacher was next to her. In the back were the two Frenchmen in white gloves and top hats and carrying canes. They waved enthusiastically.

Annabel Lee jumped down and threw herself in his arms. "And you're all right!"

"But how did you get here?"

"In the balloon," said Annabel Lee. "The balloon came back and they brought us here. Peter Drummond is looking for a ship to England and he bought us those bees for a wedding present."

"Bees?" said Morgan James. It was beginning to be too much.

"They're in the back and very fierce, too. That's why I have my bee bonnet. And it will be like a veil, too, when we get married, because I brought the Preacher who's going to do it right now."

Annabel Lee turned to wave at the Preacher and socked General Andrew Jackson right in the chest.

"And who is this woman, sir?" he said, looking at Morgan James.

Morgan James wanted to say that he had never seen her before — or just disappear.

"We're going to be married," said Annabel Lee, "right now."

"Take her to the Rear," said the General to the soldiers with him. And then he added firmly, "Right now."

They tore Annabel Lee from Morgan James. She wept and cried. "If you get yourself killed I'll never speak to you again. You don't love me."

Morgan James stood firm and brave. He hoped he radiated the resoluteness outside that he didn't feel inside.

The Frenchmen presented themselves to the General.

"Citoyens de la France, mon General," said the Fat One.

"Citizens of France, General, at your service," said the Thin One.

"Military men," said the General.

"Chasseur de la Garde," said the Fat One and ran to one of the cannons. He made the motion of lighting the charge and, putting his hands over his ears, shrieked *"Ka-Boom!"*

"Artillery," said the Thin One.

"You may take your position with your compatriot General Lafitte on the left."

Morgan James brought the bee wagon up right behind the cotton bales. He found that the view was even better from on top of the bee crates, and the angry buzzing of the bees below his feet added a wonderful exciting dimension to the wonderful exciting morning.

"Could it be Morgan James?" said a voice behind him. It was Dr. Coffin.

"The last time I saw you, you were standing up in your wagon hollering at your horse to get away from those poor miserable Indians."

"The horse was running away," said Dr. Coffin. "I was trying to stop him."

"If you believe that," said Morgan James, "you'd believe that pigs could fly."

Dr. Coffin shook his head sadly. "I'm afraid you've changed, Morgan James."

"I hope so," said Morgan James, "or I'm not going to get through this day."

"It's going to be a Day all right," said Dr. Coffin. He took out a paper from his breast pocket and read: "It was dawn on January 8th 1815 when the veterans of Wellington's Army came out of the Cypress Swamp to attack the small but gallant Forces of General Andrew Jackson in the mist before New Orleans."

"You mean it's in the papers already?" asked Morgan James as he tried to see what was going on in the fog beyond.

"That's the first sentence of my Report from the Battle Field of New Orleans for the *Nashville Courier*. I'm their correspondent on the scene."

"You mean they hired you?"

"Well, not yet, but they will when they get this Report. And you know who I just saw back at the Headquarters?"

"Who?"

"That red-haired girl I warned you about once. She was there making bandages. It's a bad sign. It's a very bad sign. She could bring misfortune to our whole adventure."

"Annabel Lee! You saw Annabel Lee? Is she all right?"

Dr. Coffin's eyes narrowed. "So that's how it is?"

"That's how it is," said Morgan James.

The rockets were coming in a steady stream of red roar from the British Lines. They roared over harmlessly and burst well behind them.

But Dr. Coffin was anxious to talk. "You know the Kentucky boys — they're on the far left — they go out every night hunting and bring back British pickets. Well, I was talking to this prisoner, and anyway, he was telling me how the British do one of their generals if he gets killed. They gut him just like you would a deer and then they put the body in a barrel of rum and send it back to England to be buried. He said the British are real fond of generals that get killed, especially if they lost the battle. What do you think of that?"

"I can't see anything out there yet," said Morgan James.

"He said that this British General Pakensomething told them they'd be in New Orleans two weeks ago. And this fellow who was talking said that he'd rather fight Napoleon, which is what he's been doing, than Jackson. And he came right from Europe. And he says that these Kentucky boys are like cats the way they prowl in the night. It's all going in my Report."

The mist was clearing now. And through his telescope Morgan James could see the first figures appearing at the far edge of the plain and he could hear the first rhythmic bleating of bagpipes. And then just as the sun burnt through he saw the figures suddenly formed into a long disciplined line.

"They come," he shouted to the General.

"I'm going," said Dr. Coffin.

And they came. The 93rd Highland Regiment came with kilts swinging and the bagpipes playing. The cannon opened on both sides. The smoke and dust filled the air, but still the Highlanders came in unbroken line.

Morgan James never knew what really happened next but a British ball hit a cotton bale and knocked it aside and the horses on the bee wagon bolted. Morgan James suddenly found himself careening toward the Highland line hanging on for dear life. He got so close he could see the pattern of the plaid and then — the wagon crashed — a great buzzing in his ears and head, and then silence.

The bee crates burst open. The bees attacked the 93rd Highland Regiment with a vengeance, face and hands and worst of all up and under the kilts. The line broke and fled. The charge was over. The battle was over. The War was over.

They brought Morgan James back from the field face down across a horse. The Frenchmen stood solemnly with top hats pressed across their stomachs and heads bowed. "Take him to his lady," said General Andrew Jackson and saluted as the limp body went by.

Annabel Lee ran to him and knelt by his side. "Speak to me, my Love," she cried. But he did not speak. The Preacher shook his head when she looked at him and searched the sky for a Rising. "Oh, my Love, come back to me," she cried. She took his hand. Her warm tears covered his hand.

"Bite it," Morgan James said. "Bite it."

THE END